Drug Lords 3

Ghost

Lock Down Publications and Ca$h Presents

Drug Lords 3

A Novel by *Ghost*

Lock Down Publications
P.O. Box 870494
Mesquite, Tx 75187

Visit our website @
www.lockdownpublications.com

Lock Down Publications
Like our page on Facebook: Lock Down Publications @
www.facebook.com/lockdownpublications.ldp
Cover design and layout by: **Dynasty Cover Me**
Book interior design by: **Shawn Walker**
Edited by: **Sunny Giovanni**

Stay Connected with Us!

Text **LOCKDOWN** to 22828 to stay up-to-date with new releases, sneak peaks, contests and more…

Thank you.

Submission Guideline.

Submit the first three chapters of your completed manuscript to ldpsubmissions@gmail.com, subject line: Your book's title. The manuscript must be in a .doc file and sent as an attachment. Document should be in Times New Roman, double spaced and in size 12 font. Also, provide your synopsis and full contact information. If sending multiple submissions, they must each be in a separate email.

Have a story but no way to send it electronically? You can still submit to LDP/Ca$h Presents. Send in the first three chapters, written or typed, of your completed manuscript to:

LDP: Submissions Dept
Po Box 870494
Mesquite, Tx 75187

DO NOT send original manuscript. Must be a duplicate.

Provide your synopsis and a cover letter containing your full contact information.

Only if your submission is **approved**, will you then get a response letter.

Thanks for considering LDP and Ca$h Presents.

DEDICATIONS:

First of all, this book is dedicated to my Baby Girl 3/10, the love of my life and purpose for everything I do. As long as I'm alive, you'll never want nor NEED for anything. We done went from flipping birds to flipping books. The best is yet to come.

To LDP'S CEO- Ca$h & COO- Shawn:

I would like to thank y'all for this opportunity. The wisdom, motivation, and encouragement that I've received from you two is greatly appreciated.

The grind is real. The loyalty in this family is real. I'm riding with LDP 'til the wheels fall off.

THE GAME IS OURS !

I GOT THE STREETS !

Ghost

Chapter 1

Sasha pressed the .40 Glock firmer into the back of Montana's head. She swallowed her spit. She could feel her heart pounding in her chest. Her eyes were bucked wide open, though the lids threatened to close because of the effects of the Rebirth. She was so high that her head was spinning. This had been her first time holding a gun in her hand, and she was both nervous and afraid. She had yet to place her index finger over the trigger from fear that the gun would go off and take Montana's life. She tangled her fingers into Montana's hair more aggressively and pulled.

Montana winced in pain. "Bitch, you ain't gotta pull on my ma'fuckin' hair like that. I ain't goin' nowhere." She hissed, trying to yank her head away.

Stevo took the shotgun off of his lap and rested the barrel against Montana's cheek. "Bitch, you actin' real tough for somebody that's seconds away from having their noodles in their lap. You might wanna simmer yo' monkey ass down a lil' bit." Stevo kept the weapon pressed against her face while he drove with one hand. "Now all this shit can go real smooth as long as you cooperate." He pressed the barrel harder against her cheek. It began to cut into her skin, forming a red ring around it. "You hear me?"

Montana opened her eyes and trailed them over until she was looking at him. "Stevo, I don't know what has gotten into you, but you know this shit ain't right. You and I have been like brother and sister ever since we were kids. What the fuck are you doin'?"

Stevo looked back to Sasha. "Say, shorty, if this bitch act like she tryin' to do too much, you knock her ma'fuckin' head off. You hear me?"

Sasha nodded. "Yes, daddy. I hear you loud and clear." She sounded as if she were confident in following through on his commands. In actuality, she was terrified. She had never killed anybody before, and she didn't even know how to work the gun. On top of that, she didn't want to kill Montana. She didn't want to go to hell for an eternity. She prayed that Montana played everything cool. She didn't want her death on her hands.

Montana frowned. "I never thought I would see the day where you betray my brother, Stevo. Makaroni crazy about yo' ass. This how you do him? And my mother for that matter?"

Stevo laughed. "Bitch, this shit ain't personal, it's just business. Besides, if anything happens to you, Makaroni will never find out who did it. I couldn't hurt my nigga like that. Maisey either. You're just a victim of muthafuckin' circumstance. Deal wit' it." He took the exit ramp off the freeway. "What you think she finna be doing when we get here?" Stevo asked.

Montana felt Sasha tightening her grip on her hair. She clenched her teeth. It felt like Sasha was pulling the roots slowly out of her scalp. "Stevo, that girl was tired and hungry. She is probably sleep."

"You didn't tell her where you were going?" He wanted to know.

"N'all, I just told her that I was going to work, and that she could make herself comfortable. I told her that I would be back later on tonight. She didn't ask me where I worked or nothin' like that." Montana winced as Sasha tightened her grip again. "Bitch, could you please cut me some slack? You pullin' my fuckin' hair out of my head."

"Bitch, this sewed in. This shit ain't yours. You'll be awright." Sasha returned dryly. Sasha wanted to seem tough.

She figured that acting as she pulled on Montana's hair, and keeping a good grip on it, would stop Montana from getting the idea to do anything else that would force her to have to use the gun.

"Yousa petty bitch I see. You don't even know me, and you treatin' me like this? Trust me, you gon' get yours." Montana promised.

Sasha pressed the gun into the back of her neck. "Is that a threat? Huh?"

Montana kept her silence. She didn't want to provoke Sasha any more than she probably had. She knew that her best bet was to keep her comments, and her thoughts to herself. The only way she could possibly get out of the situation that she was in, was if she used her street smarts.

Stevo laughed and looked back to Sasha again. "Girl it seem like you turning into yo daddy. I like seeing that shit." He laughed louder. "On my word, I'ma turn yo lil' ass into a killa just like me. Then, when it comes down to me crushing bitches, I can just have you do it on my behalf. You said you wanted that number one slot, right?" He looked back out at the road.

"Yes, daddy. But I thought I already had that?" Sasha was confused.

"It's day by day. Just like I gotta get my ass up and trap every day to make sure that I stay on top of the Game, bitch, you gotta do the same thing under this regiment. Ain't no such thang as you having one good day, and you thanking that's supposed to carry you from then on out. The Game don't work like that for me, and it don't work like that for you. Now, rip that shit out her head if you have to. Make that bitch honor you like you honor me." He snapped.

Sasha yanked so hard on Montana's hair that it pulled twenty strands from the root. They began to bleed right away. "Bitch, hold still before I pull this trigger."

Montana bit her tongue to prevent herself from cursing both Stevo and Sasha out. She hated them both. She wanted to get her hands on Sasha. She knew that if she had the opportunity, she was going to beat her senseless. Instead of opening her mouth to make her situation worse, she remained calm, and imagined her mother Maisey's beautiful face. She had always raised her to be strong. To be a fighter. To never fold under any circumstances. She thought about the things that Maisey had told her that she'd been forced to endure while held prisoner by Stacy. That both sickened her and gave Montana strength to overcome her current situation.

Stevo turned off of busy 27th Street and took Chambers Street until he made a left on 28th and Chambers. He read the addresses. "Bitch, which house is the one you staying at?"

"2951." Montana relayed to him. "After you get this lil' girl, what are you goin' to do with me? I ain't got nothin' to do with any of this. I'm caught in the fuckin' middle."

Stevo smiled. "Shorty, long as she up here we good. I'ma let you go." He lied. He had already set his mind on killing Montana and cutting her body up into little biddy pieces. Once she was cut up, he would dump here body into the river where nobody would ever find her.

"So, you just gone let me go then?" Montana found that hard to believe. She already knew about Stevo's reputation as a cold-blooded killer. Makaroni was just as cold. Stevo had to know that she would go back and tell Makaroni what he'd done to her. When she did, Makaroni was sure to go crazy. She couldn't see Stevo being dumb enough to let her simply go. That worried her.

"Yep. Regardless of what you may think about me, I still look at you as my sister. I could never hurt you unless you made me. Long as Kandace is up there, and I get her, I ain't gon' lay a finger on you. You got my word on that." He pulled into the long alley that was behind the duplex that Montana pointed out to him. Once there, he parked his truck two houses down from it. He cut the ignition and looked over at Montana. "Look, sis, I'm sorry for hurting you. Like I said before, this shit is just business. It ain't nothin' personal. The sooner you understand that, the better off you will be."

Montana nodded her head as best she could. She had so much hate in her heart for Stevo that it made her sweat under her armpits. "It's all good, Stevo. Just go up there and get her the fuck out of my house, and then gon' head on about yo business. I'll keep this shit between me and you. Makaroni ain't gotta know nothin'."

Stevo smiled. "That's a girl." His smile slowly turned into an evil glare. "You finna come up here with me though. I don't know shit about this house, and you do. Come on." He poked her in the ribs with the shotgun. "Baby, let her hair go."

Sasha followed his command. "You want me to come too?"

Stevo shook his head. "N'all bitch, you stay put. I need you to get behind the steering wheel. As soon as you see me come down the alley with Kandace, you start the truck and get ready to pull off. You understand that?"

Sasha nodded. "Okay, daddy. Please don't be all day."

***

Montana fit the key into the lock and twisted it. The back door clicked. She pushed it in. She heard the sounds of

Summer Walker singing through the speakers. She and Kandace had been listening to her new *Over It* album before she left. Stevo grabbed her by the neck. He pressed his lip to her earlobe. "Bitch, which one of these rooms was she sleeping in before you left?"

Montana felt her stomach turn. She hated the scent of Stevo's breath. She hated feeling his heat on her skin. "The middle room. That's my room. She was laying in the bed before I left."

"Cool. Remember, just be cool, sis. This shit ain't got nothin' to do with you. I'ma take her with me and you go back to doing whatever you were doing before you bumped into her on Twenty-Seventh. Awright?"

"Yeah."

"Come on." Stevo threw her in front of him. "Call that hoe."

"Kandace? Girl, I'm back. Where you at?" Montana called.

Stevo crept down the hallway looking from right to left. It smelled like jasmine. The house was warm and cozy. Fully carpeted. He stepped past the bathroom door and nudged it open. Empty. He pushed Montana ahead a bit more. "Which room you say again?"

Montana pointed at the center room. The door was slightly ajar. "Dis one right here."

Stevo flung her to the floor. "Don't get yo ass up until I tell you to." He cocked the shotgun, and slowly opened the door. He held his breath to ensure that he could hear every bit of noise. The door creaked open. He stepped through it. His eyes lit up with excitement when he saw the bundle under the blankets of Montana's bed. Kandace's shoes were on the side of it. He smiled. He bit into his bottom lip. *Yeah I got this lil' bitch now*, he thought. He crept closer to the bed.

When he was standing beside it, he pressed the barrel of the shotgun to where he figured Kandace's head would be. He leaned down and took a hold of the blanket. With one flip he pulled it backward ready to shoot. "Bitch get yo ass up!" He ordered.

Kandace pushed open the closet door and rushed him. *Boom! Boom! Boom! Boom!* The bullets threw Stevo into the air. He landed into the window, shattering the glass. He dropped the shotgun and stood frozen as he felt the excruciating pain in his back. He turned around to face Kandace. "Bitch, I'm finna kill you."

Kandace's face was a mug of hatred. She held the .9 millimeter in her hand with the barrel smoking. "Oh, yeah? Well, I wanna see you try." *Boom! Boom! Boom! Boom!* Stevo flew out of the window. He landed on his back hard. Kandace rushed to the window to look down at his unmoving body. "Punk ass nigga. I ain't Keaira!" She screamed.

Montana rushed into the room. "Did you get his punk ass? Huh?"

Kandace nodded. "Yeah. I hid in the closet just like you told me to. The way you made up the bed tricked his goofy ass, too. He went right for it, and I popped him up. He got what he deserved." She said defeated. She couldn't help but to think about her sister Keaira. She wished she were still alive. She missed her. The remorse of her death was starting to effect Kandace more and more. If she had never started to mess with Stevo behind her back, Keaira would still be alive. She was sure of that.

Montana hugged her. "I gotta see this for myself. I can't believe that devil is finally dead." She kissed the side of Kandace's head, and stepped away from her. She stepped on the glass that was all over the floor along with broken chips of wood. Blood decorated the walls, and floor as well. Montana stepped over all of it to look out of the window. She looked down and prepared herself to see a twisted version of Stevo. What she saw nearly took her breath away. "Uh, Kandace, where is he?"

Kandace stood in the middle other floor with her gun held at her side. "What?"

"Stevo, he ain't out there. You sure you shot him?" Montana grew worried.

"Yeah, I hit his ass every bit of eight times. I watched the holes form in his clothes. What the fuck you mean?" She rushed to the window, pushing Montana to the side. The empty sight brought her to her knees. "Holy fuck. We gotta get the hell out of here."

"I agree; let's go!" Montana yelled.

Chapter 2

Cassidy heard the cocking of Seth's .380. She grew cold. Chill bumps peered all over her body. "What did you say to me?" She slowly turned around to face her husband. The sight of the chrome weapon being pointed at her was enough to put her on edge. She could smell the alcohol on Seth's breath.

"I said I know that you stepping out on me with that lil' boy. How could you? How could you ruin our family for a child?" He shook as he held the gun. After their home was burned to the ground, he'd gotten laid off his job. Financially, they had been taken through the ringer. He felt less than a man. He'd been unable to give his family a new home they could call their own. He felt worse than scum. Then to catch Cassidy in the act with a kid they had both taken part in help raising, he felt betrayed and emasculated. "How could you do this to our family? How?" He snapped.

Cassidy backed up with her hands raised. "Seth, you are real drunk right now. I can smell your breath. You need to calm down. You're talking about some stuff that never happened." She lied. The truth was that she'd slept with her son's right-hand man on more than one occasion. There was something about sleeping with Makaroni that made her feel vibrant and youthful. It felt good to be desired by a man half her age. She didn't want to apologize about that. Even though Seth was her husband, she felt like she didn't owe him any explanations. She had fallen out of love a long time ago.

"You're a liar. I watched you and him together. Don't fuckin' lie to me!" He hollered. "Admit it, Cass. Admit it, or so help me God, I'm going to kill you right here."

Cassidy closed her eyes and took a deep breath. Her hands remained in the air. Seth was always harder to reason with whenever he drank. His reasoning was at its lowest point. He had only hit her twenty times throughout their relationship. Each time he had done so, he had been drunk like she assumed he was at this moment. "Seth, please calm down. Now, I would never step out on you with nobody. You should know me better than that by now. I love you way to—"

Slap!

"Liar!" Seth backhanded her so hard that she flew into Maisey's china cabinet.

Both of her hands went through the glass. She pulled them back bloody. She sank to her ass, the pain from the shards of glass resonating with her now. Blood dripped from her elbows.

Seth grabbed her by the blouse and pulled her up. He flung her into the wall. "Tell me the truth, Cassidy. Tell me right now or I swear I'm going to kill you."

Maisey jerked awake at the hearing of Cassidy crashing into her china cabinet. She hopped out of bed and grabbed her baseball bat. The first thing that came to her mind was that Stacy was back to get her. She refused to let this happen again. She would rather die than to be held prisoner by him again. Images of the sexually grotesque things that he had done to her played in her mind like a movie. She tightened her hands around the bat and tip toed out of the room.

"Okay, Seth. I slept with him." Cassidy was in pain. She just wanted it to all be over with. She had to find a way to mentally capture Seth. She needed to penetrate his mind. If she could do that, then she could turn the unfortunate situation in her favor.

"Who, Cassidy? Who did you sleep with?" He held his hand around her throat without applying any pressure. He wanted to kill her, but he loved her so much. For so long she had been his world. But every time he imagined her touching Makaroni, or him touching her, it made him want to cause her the most amount of pain. He wanted her to feel the same level of agony that he was feeling. "Who?"

"Makaroni. I slept with him. I'm sorry, Seth. I just been so lost. I didn't know what to do, or where to turn. I'm so, so sorry." She squeezed her eyelids to make water come out of them. But nothing came. She hated herself for being so strong when she needed to be weak.

He placed the gun into the small of his back. Seth grabbed her by the throat and choked her as hard as he could. "I knew you slept with him. I knew it. Oh, I hate you so much! I hate you so fuckin' much!" He squeezed with all of his strength. He was dead set on killing her. He would be able to go on with his life after there was no more breath in her body. He would kill her, then he would track down and do the same to Makaroni. "I hate you, Cassidy. Bitch, you gotta die. I'ma kill you and Makaroni black ass." He swore. He was choking so hard that his fingers were popping. He imagined her laying in a coffin, lifeless. He grew giddy. He saw the cemetery. He saw the grave plots. Hers would be right beside Makaroni's. This made him elated. Endorphins released inside of his brain. He picked Cassidy up into the air with two hands and slammed her to the floor. He straddled her, still choking.

"Ahhhhhhhh!" *Clunk!* Maisey slammed the bat as hard as she could on top of Seth's head. It split like a busted pumpkin, splattering blood everywhere.

He continued to choke Cassidy. The Jack Daniels that he'd drank blocked the physical pain from taking effect. His hatred fueled him to press forward.

Maisey took a step back. "Get off of her!" She swung the bat sideways and slammed it into his left eye socket.

He released Cassidy and jumped up screaming in pain. He held his hand over the shattered eye socket. "Arrgh! Arrgh! I can't see! I can't see!" He fell to his knees.

Cassidy scooted backward on her ass. She struggled to breathe. Her arms continued to drip blood. She got up and stood behind Maisey. "Thank you, girl. Now, what do we do?"

"Seth, get the hell out of my house. You ain't welcome here no more. Get out or I'm gon' hit you again." She promised.

Seth flew backward into the wall, still holding his bleeding eye. The gun fell to the ground. Blood dripped from him at a steady pace. "Why did you hit me, Maisey? Dis ain't got shit to do with you."

Cassidy ran over and grabbed the gun from the floor. "Get out of here, Seth. Please leave. I don't wanna shoot you. Please just go." She begged.

Seth staggered to his feet. He used the wall to guide him toward the front door. He left a trail of blood along it. "This shit ain't over. It ain't over. I swear I'ma be back for both of y'all." He fell to the front door. He pulled it open and left into the night.

Cassidy let lout a sigh of relief. She slumped to her ass. "Girl, you need to get me to the hospital. I don't know how much blood I lost, but I'm dizzy."

Maisey fell to her knees beside her. "I got you. Just hold on."

***

Phoenix stood back and watched Jahliya's mansion explode in flames. The flickering of the fire glossed across his eyes. He could feel the heat from the blaze. He held his Assault Rifle at the ready. Anybody that ran out of the palace was sure to be gunned down. He and his Duffel Bag Cartel crew had each section of the mansion blocked off. Nobody was getting out of it without them being spotted and riddled with bullets. Phoenix was ready for the war. He was tired of losing money to JaMichael and his off-brand dope boys. The sooner he killed him, the sooner he could take over the Rebirth and solidify himself as a true Drug Lord. Rubio Flores would have to fully invest within the Duffel Bag Cartel. That meant millions for he and his crew. Millions that Phoenix had to have.

JaMichael wrapped his arm around Jahliya's waist and bid her to run faster. His chest felt tight. His throat was drier than a desert in the summertime. His Balenciaga's beat against the concrete of the tunnel as he jogged beside his sister. "Come on baby, we almost to the other end."

Jahliya tried her best to keep up. She could feel the heat from the blast of the fires from up above. She was thankful that the high definition cameras had picked up Phoenix and his crew. As soon as Phoenix and his Duffel Bag Cartel members hopped the fence, the censors went off and alerted Jahliya that there were intruders present. She watched on the camera as they surrounded her palace. The infrared cameras even honed in on the grenades that the intruders were strapped with. As soon as they were detected, she alerted JaMichael and Makaroni.

Makaroni jogged close behind. He had both Glocks in his hand. The tunnel was narrow, and swampy. It smelled stale. Bats flew up and down it. There was water under his feet that splashed as they ran. "Man, why the fuck is we running if you know for a fact that it's Phoenix back there? That shit don't make no sense."

"Bruh, if you want me to go back, I'll go back and handle my business." DaBaby assured him. He jogged behind them with a Mach .90 in his hand. He was ready to use it. Ready to do some damage. He couldn't believe that the Duffel Bag Cartel was coming at them with grenades. That excited him to a strange point.

"N'all we gon' follow them for now. I wanna see what JaMichael finna do." Makaroni told him. He made sure that he stayed on JaMichael and Jahliya's heels.

JaMichael came out of the tunnel. It was pitch black. The tunnel led to a riverbank that was only a block away from Jahliya's palace. To the right of the riverbank was a parked Yukon Denali. He jogged to it and opened the door for Jahliya. Once he had her in safe and sound, he popped the locks for Makaroni and his crew. They all got in and slammed the doors one after another. JaMichael got behind the wheel and stormed away.

Makaroni sat in his seat fuming. "What the fuck is the game plan? Huh? What the fuck are we about to do? I know we ain't gon' just let this shit ride. This ma'fucka could've blew us the fuck up!" He snapped.

"Makaroni, calm down. Getting yourself all riled up ain't gon' help the situation at all. We need to come up with a plan that will be smart. It look like Phoenix done got his hands on some military shit." Jahliya pulled her seat belt around her.

"That's all the fuck we been doing is being calm. When do we say fuck being calm and go at this nigga's ass? Huh?" Makaroni asked.

"On some real shit, I wanna handle that nigga tonight. It's like the homie said, he could've blew all of our asses to smithereens tonight. We lucky that Jahliya software picked up all of that shit, or we would've been assed out." DaBaby added.

"Aw, we gon' get his ass. You betta believe that. Let me just drop my sister off somewhere that I know she can be safe. Once she good, then we can go bomb on some shit tonight." JaMichael was heated. He felt like Phoenix was punking him. He didn't like for no man making him feel like a bitch. Phoenix had a habit of making him feel just like that. He kept imagining how the ground felt shaking as the mansion exploded above them. They had gotten out of the top portion and into the underground bunker a split second before the top half of the palace blew up. All five of them had been thrown to the ground from the mighty blast. JaMichael slammed his hand on to the steering wheel. "Dat bitch ass nigga gotta go. He gotta fuckin' go!"

Jahliya rubbed his back. "Y'all gon' get his ass. Trust me. Y'all gon' get him good. I already know that."

Makaroni sighed dejectedly. "Fuck dat shit, Jahliya. Yo, if this nigga JaMichael don't get his shit together real soon, I'm taking over this war. Ma'fuckas gon' have to fall behind me. That's how that's gon' go."

"You ain't taking over shit, lil' nigga. This my city. This my beef. I got this." JaMichael let it be known.

"Don't seem like it. Seems to me that Phoenix is treating you like a pussy. Because I'm rolling behind yo simple ass, he treating me and my niggas, too. I don't like for no nigga thinking he fuckin' me over. That roll over shit ain't in me, JaMichael. I'm a ma'fuckin' killa. No mercy type shit. Now, get yo shit together or we out. It's as simple as that. I'm this close to saying fuck Rubio Flores after I say fuck you. Blood or no blood." Makaroni felt his chest heaving. He was amped up.

JaMichael clenched his jaw. "Nigga, you need to calm yo ignorant ass down and let me handle this shit. Like I said before, I'll take care of the shit down here. I ain't ask you or no niggas to come. Y'all came on your own volition."

"Nigga, you talking like that, I'll go back to the Mill. Fuck Memphis." Makaroni was over it.

JaMichael looked back at him. "You ain't saying shit. I'll drop you niggas back off at yo whip. Fuck y'all. I'll see you when I see you."

"JaMichael? What are you doin'? We need them. Who else can we really trust?" Jahliya asked.

"Man, fuck them. I don't need no nigga. I can handle Phoenix on my own. That nigga ain't no ma'fuckin' God. These niggas wanna leave, they can leave. That's on every-thang, Shawty."

"Yo, you ain't gotta be talking that tough Tony shit to me, homeboy. Don't forget, me and my nigga saved yo life. I already see you don't know what the fuck you doing down here." DaBaby said, getting heated. He was starting to not like JaMichael.

"You know. Y'all gotta go. I'm dropping you niggas back off at yo whip, Makaroni. Y'all can head back up north. I don't need nan' one of y'all. I'll handle this shit on my own."

"JaMichael, are you sure?" Jahliya asked. After watching Phoenix release grenades, she was worried. She didn't think her brother could hold his own against the Duffel Bag Cartel. Phoenix was well connected and lethal. She worried that he would outthink and annihilate JaMichael. After all, he had been trapping longer.

"You muthafuckin' right I'm sure." Though these were the words that came out of his mouth, he wasn't as sure as he made himself out to be. It had been a while since he had been in an all-out war. Phoenix had the upper hand, and there was a lot at stake and not a lot of time.

"Well, if that's how you're feeling, JaMichael, then we up out of here. Y'all heard that? We back to Milwaukee to-night." Makaroni sat back and closed his eyes.

"Even though I don't know if I like you, JaMichael, for the right price I'll stay on and a head bussah for you." DaBaby offered.

JaMichael looked him over from his rear-view mirror. "What's up?"

"Shid, I roll under Stevo, not Makaroni. He told me to stay down here until the job was done. I'm saying money talks. You drop that bread and put me in with some of those thick ass Memphis girls then we got a deal."

Roscoe interrupted. "Don't forget about me, Shorty. You already know that if you finna stay down here then I am, too. We do everything together. Besides, who gon' have yo back betta than me?"

DaBaby turned back to JaMichael. "Yo, make that a contract for two. Makaroni gon' go back to Milwaukee. Me and Roscoe gon' stay down here and handle business for you. What do you say?"

JaMichael looked over to Jahliya. She shrugged. Then he looked to Makaroni. "Dawg, you cool wit' this?"

Makaroni ignored him. He was too busy reading a text from Montana.

Montana: Get home. Stevo tried to kill me. Hurry please!!!

"Yo get me back to my whip. I don't give a fuck what these niggas do. Hurry the fuck up."

"We'll discuss business once I drop this nigga off." JaMichael told DaBaby and Roscoe.

Jahliya lowered her head and placed her hand over her forehead. "JaMichael, I hope you know what you're doing. I really do."

"I got this," was his only reply.

Ghost

Chapter 3

It was a sunny and breezy day the next afternoon. Makaroni rolled into the city of Milwaukee with a frown. He was driving with one hand reading text after text from both Montana and Maisey. He was pissed. He felt that he hadn't been away from Milwaukee long enough for things to have spiraled out of control the way they had. His mother told him that Seth had gotten drunk and tried to kill Cassidy. She was in the hospital getting medical attention. Montana told him how Stevo put his hands on her, and how she felt that she was sure he would have killed her if Kandace hadn't stepped in to take him out. His mind was spinning. He didn't know which problem to address first. On top of that, Stevo wasn't answering any of his texts. He hit him up over and over on Facebook as well. He saw that Stevo hadn't been on it in a few days.

Makaroni stepped on the gas and pulled up in front of Maisey's home ten minutes later. Before he could park all the way, he saw Montana coming down the stairs of the porch. She hurried to the passenger's door and pulled on the handle. He popped the locks for her.

Montana slid into the seat. "Bruh, pull off before mama even wake up. I gotta tell you what the fuck is going on before she get to bombarding you with all of that other Cassidy ass drama." She rolled her eyes.

Makaroni drove away from the curb. "What's good, Montana? What the fuck is up with Stevo?"

She sighed. "He done snapped. He fuckin' lil' girls. He been pimping them and all kinds of shit. According to Kandace, he killed one of them because they no longer wanted to work for him. She say he killed Keaira, too. I don't know how true that is, but ain't nobody heard from her ever since they got into it a few weeks ago. He was out of order for how he did me though." She winced in pain and leaned her head back so he could see her neck.

Makaroni continued to drive. He glanced over a few times. He made out the red marks around Montana's neck. "What he do, choke you or somethin'?"

She nodded. "He did more than that. He put a gun to my head, and choke slammed me to the ground. I thought he broke a few of my ribs, but luckily he didn't. The doctor said that they are bruised really bad. He acted like he was going to rape me, too." Montana wanted to lay it on thick. She knew that Makaroni and Stevo had been right hand men ever since they were children. She felt their bond was nearly unbreakable.

Makaroni felt sick, and then anger coursed through him as he imagined Stevo manhandling his sister and trying to rape her. The image was enough to make his blood pressure rise. He pulled the truck over. "Bring yo ass over here."

Montana didn't hesitate. She closed the distance between them and straddled his lap. She hugged him with tears in her eyes. "I know if you were here, he would have never tried any of this dumb shit. I hate him so much, Makaroni. That nigga ain't right." She held her brother as tight as she could.

"It's all good, lil' sis. I'ma holler at that nigga. We gon' get all of this shit straightened out. I promise." He didn't know how to feel or what to think. Stevo was like his brother. They had done everything together. He was praying that it had all been one big misunderstanding. He was hoping that Stevo had been drunk, and even quite possibly gone off of the Rebirth. That he wasn't in his right mind. He couldn't fathom that Stevo would ever try to hurt Montana when he knew how much she meant to him.

Montana sat back and looked into his eyes. "I missed you, Mack. I swear to God I been going crazy missing you. I thought I was never goin' to see you again. Especially when he got to talking that murder talk." She laid her face in the crux of his neck. His cologne drifted up her nostrils. She felt secure. She felt safe. She hugged him tighter.

Makaroni pulled her back just a tad until their noses were brushed up against each other's. He looked into her beautiful brown eyes and rubbed her curls. "I'm back now. I got you, Montana. You already know that I missed you like a ma'fucka, too." He kissed her lips softly at first. Then he added more pressure.

Montana moaned and closed her eyes. She felt his strong arms wrapped around her small frame. She felt so protected. She gave into his kisses. Her lips sought his. Then their tongues were dancing upon each other's. Makaroni rubbed all over her back. He gripped her ass and held her firmer to him.

"What is mama talking about?" He asked breaking their kiss.

Montana rubbed his lips with her thumbs. Her red Maybelline lipstick left traces all over his. "Seth supposedly found out about you and Cassidy, which is crazy because I didn't even know there was a you and Cassidy to find out about." Montana grew angry. "When did that shit start?"

Makaroni tapped her on the side of her ass. She slid off of his lap and back into the passenger's seat. "I fucked with Cassidy a few times, but it ain't shit serious. Every young nigga my age love that vet pussy. Including myself. It's things that an older woman can do that young females ain't learned yet."

Montana felt offended. "Like what?" She wanted to know. She wondered if Makaroni knew that every word he spoke in regards to another woman made her sensitive and quick to anger. Even though he was her brother, she felt some type of way about him. There was something going on inside of herself that wanted to possess him. She wanted to be stingy. She didn't want to share him with anybody outside of their mother. She hated herself for feeling like that because she was sure that he didn't feel the same.

Makaroni laid back in the driver's seat with a smile on his face. He didn't honestly know how to break things down to Montana in a way that she would understand. He didn't want to hurt her feelings. He knew that she could be sensitive at times when it came to him. "Look, sis, I don't wanna get into all of that. It's pointless. The bottom line is that it's true. She and I had been fucking around. It is what it is."

"N'all, fuck that. Makaroni, I remember a time when you and I were the best of friends. We never kept secrets from one another, and we spoke uncut about everything. Don't coddle me. Keep that shit real. I'm woman enough to see where you are coming from. I wanna know what makes older women so much better than me."

"I didn't say they were better than you in particular. I said that most young niggas my age love to have a vet bitch ducked off somewhere. Older women are just different."

"Mack, you steady saying that, but you ain't telling me how. For one, Cassidy ain't even got a pot to piss in. You could've at least went out and got you an older woman that got something going for herself." She rolled her eyes.

"It ain't about all of that, Montana."

"Den she practically raised yo ass. She just like our mother. How could you even see her in that sexual light? That's just weird."

"Really?" Makaroni raised his eyebrow. "You wanna throw that weird word in there? You was just sitting on my lap, kissing all over my lips. What? You don't think the shit we do is weird?"

"Hell n'all. You're my brother. Don't nobody love you like I do. I don't give a fuck what the world say when it comes to how we feel about each other. I bet ain't none of the naysayers gon' hold us down like we hold each other down. Will they?"

Makaroni shook his head. "N'all, they won't."

"Awright then? Fuck them. Now back to this bitch. What's so good about her?"

"Look, I like older women. I always have. I don't give a fuck that she was around ever since I was a young nigga. Shid, on some real shit, I had a thing for her back then, too. It does somethin' to me to know that I get to fuck a woman who used to be so off limits. I love that type of shit. I can't help it. Regular hoez are boring to me. If I ain't crossing some type of line, or she ain't forbidden, then I can't get on board. I don't know why I'm like this, but I am. I like forbidden pussy. Cassidy is Stevo's mother. Shid, she call me her son. That's twisted. That's why I loved fucking her though. There. Can you handle that?"

Montana shrugged. "That ain't what you made it seem like originally, but whatever. What's more off limits than your own sister though? Tell me that."

He laughed. "Shit. But this ain't about you."

"Yeah right. Nigga, you created a monster. Everything that got something to do with you is about me now. Are you still finna fuck with her even though you got me now?" She wanted to know on the one hand, and on the other she really didn't think she could handle the response if it was the wrong one.

"Sis, sooner or later you and I are going to quit fuckin'. We need to reestablish our bond. The one we had before we got to doing all this dark shit. I gotta protect you more than I been doing." He started the ignition.

Montana was taken aback. "I know you're joking right?"

Makaroni shook his head. "N'all. I love you too much to keep going in on you like that. We can love each other without fuckin'. We ain't never had to fuck in order to love each other before."

Montana crossed her arms. "So you finna shit on me for this old bitch. Really?"

"Hell n'all. You already know that ain't finna happen. You can stop that shit."

"It's all good, Makaroni. You're right. We do need to stop all the shit we been doing. I'ma fall back. Take me back to mama house. It's good."

Makaroni wanted to baby her. He knew that she was only acting out of pure emotion. She probably thought they would lose their connection if the sex stopped, but he was dead set on proving to her that it wouldn't. "Yo Montana, I love you, sis. I got yo back, and regardless, I'ma forever hold you down."

"Makaroni, on some real shit, yo voice right now is making me wanna bust you in your mouth. Just shut up. Take me to mama house so I can duck off by myself and collect my thoughts. I hate that I even crossed those lines with you now. Damn."

"I still love you. Fuck what you talking about." He returned.

"Yeah, whatever. It sure don't feel like it."

***

Maisey set a plate of barbecue baby back ribs and a glass of pink lemonade in front of Makaroni. "So, baby, that's basically what happened. I bust his head pretty good, too. He ran out of here bleeding, swearing up and down that me and

Cassidy was gon' get what we had coming. I ain't seen him since, but I'd be lying to you if I said I wasn't a bit worried."

Makaroni looked up to her with hatred in his eyes. "That nigga ever come around you again, I'ma stank his ass in cold blood. Excuse my language. Ain't nobody gon' put they hands on my mother, or my sister. Cassidy neither." He snapped.

Maisey hugged his neck. She kissed his cheek. "I ain't worried about it now that you back in town. Everybody know how crazy my baby is." She kissed his cheek again. She walked around the table and sat across from him, staring.

Makaroni took a sip from his lemonade. He put it down and she was still staring at him. "What's good, mama?"

She smiled, then blushed. She really didn't know how she was going to ask him what she needed to without feeling awkward, so she just blurted it out. "Boy, what the hell were you and Cassidy doing sleeping together? Were you trying to break up their marriage?"

"N'all, mama, it wasn't nothin' like that. It just happened."

"Has it happened since they been living under my roof?" She could only imagine what that must have been like. She hoped that she wasn't in the house while it was taking place.

"Seriously, mama?"

"Boy, spill the beans, and you bet not lie either."

Makaroni sighed. "Yeah. We done got down since she been living here. That's my bad." He avoided her eyes.

"Sounds like it's hers, too." Maisey said out loud. "Wow. It didn't feel odd with her calling you son all the time? And you calling her mama?"

Makaroni really couldn't look at Maisey now. "Mama, come on now. You making me feel crazy as ever."

"Well, you should. Don't be calling that woman no mama, and then turn around and got yo stuff in her hours later. That's wrong, boy. That's why you can't even look at me right now."

Makaroni tried to look over at her and couldn't. He had never felt so embarrassed in all of his life. "Like I said, that's my bad."

Maisey was confused. "Boy, do you have mommy issues or something? I've heard of females having daddy issues, but I don't think I've ever heard of a male having mother issues before. I suppose that can be a thing. But was it somethin' I created? I mean, did I do somethin' wrong?" She was concerned.

"N'all, mama, you were good. It ain't got nothin' to do with you. It's just somethin' that all boys got in em'. It's real hard for me to explain. Now, can I please just eat my food? I don't wanna talk about this no more."

"Well, okay." Maisey came around the table and kissed his cheek. "Enjoy, baby. Thank you for coming home to make sure that I was okay. I sincerely appreciate that. You hear me?"

"Yes, ma'am."

She rubbed the side of his face. "I oughta kick Cassidy's ass. How would she feel if I corrupted her son?" She walked off still confused about Makaroni and Cassidy's sexual relationship.

Makaroni picked up a rib and shook his head. "What the hell I done got myself in the middle of?"

Montana waited until Maisey stepped out of the dining room and went back into her bedroom before she approached a sitting Makaroni. He had just bitten a chunk of barbecued meat off of his rib. She stepped beside him and leaned down.

"Mack, I need to talk to you downstairs when you're finished eating."

Makaroni looked up to her. "Awright." He wondered what she wanted to talk about. He was hoping that it wasn't more about Cassidy. He was already over the whole him and Cassidy thing. He didn't care what either Maisey or Montana said. If the opportunity presented itself to lay Cassidy down, he was going for it. He found her way too attractive, and the off-limits factor only heightened her appeal to him, especially since Seth was all screwed up over it. He had never liked the man for a reason he couldn't quite pinpoint.

"I'm for real, Mack. Don't slip ya ass out of here without coming downstairs to holler at me."

"I ain't. I promise that as soon as I'm done up here, I'll be down there." He sucked barbecue sauce from his fingers.

Montana couldn't help shivering. She watched his fingers pop out of his mouth. His juicy lips made her feel some type of way. She tried her best to avoid thinking anything sexual, but it felt like the more he ignored her the more she wanted him. She was irritated. "Well, okay then. I'll see you in like, what, ten minutes or somethin'?"

"Yeah, about that. I'll be down there."

"Cool." She eased away from the table.

Makaroni looked over his phone again. He found it odd that Stevo still hadn't hit him up. He was hoping that despite everything that Montana told him that Stevo was alright. He didn't know how he was going to get at him for what he'd done to his sister. He figured he'd cross that bridge when he came to it. He wanted to get down to the bottom of it. But even so, he prayed that Stevo was okay. His right-hand man was the only one that he truly trusted in the cold world. The separation was killing Makaroni.

Ghost

Chapter 4

Stevo growled in pain as Jada pulled the last gauze off of his chest wound. She placed it into the metal pan beside the bed that he was laying in. She looked over his injuries and began to properly clean them one at a time. Stevo gritted his teeth. "Man, what the fuck is the use of wearing a bullet proof vest if I still gotta go through this shit? That don't make no sense!"

Jada smiled. "You should be lucky to be alive. I don't know where you got that thing, but if you hadn't had it, I am sure that these bullets would have penetrated and possibly killed you. You were shot eight times Stevo, and you're still here. You gotta thank God for that." She continued doing what she needed to do to get him together.

Jada had been driving down 27th and Burleigh Street when she spotted Stevo staggering and bleeding. She watched him for a few moments. He made it halfway down the block and then fainted. Unwilling to just leave him there in such a horrible and drug infested neighborhood, she rushed him into the backseat of her car. Halfway through the process, he woke up hollering for her to not take him to the hospital. He said he couldn't deal with the cops. She didn't know what that meant in its entirety, but she listened. She brought him to her home where she was able to work on him herself. She was in her second year of medical school at Marquette University. His injuries were superficial enough for her to not panic. None of the rounds went deep enough for him to need further medical assistance. She was confident that she could get him back to a full one hundred percent.

"You wanna tell me how this happened again?" She asked, cleansing his front wounds with alcohol pads.

Stevo closed his eyes. He needed a shot of the Rebirth. The Rebirth would make it so that he couldn't feel anything. He had to find a way to get to his Trap house, or to contact Sasha. He'd only spoken to her once since Kandace laid him out. "Look, Shorty, I already told you. Some ma'fucka tried to rob me. You already know how them niggas get down in the Burleigh Zoo." On 27th and Burleigh where she had found him, the locals called it the Zoo because of how wild it was. The area was frivolous for serious gang activity and senseless killings. 27th and Burleigh was a hot zone for Milwaukee.

"Well, how did you get away? They don't find many victims in the Zoo that are alive. You were fortunate."

"Fortunate my ass. I'm laying here with eight slugs. You call that fortunate?" He sat up. He was feening for the Rebirth. Not only was he in pain, but he felt like his insides were being turned inside out. "Look, I need to make a call. You wanna step out of here for a minute?"

Jada placed the last gauze in place and taped it down. She nodded and took her gloves off. She was five feet six inches tall, a hundred and forty pounds. Her skin was a light caramel. Her eyes were brown, and her shoulder-length hair, permed. "You know, most people in your position would be thanking me right now. Since you've been here, all you've been is argumentative. Do you have anything positive you would like to say to me?" She asked, gathering up her things.

Stevo stood up. He looked down into her pretty face and tuned into her succulent lips. Her eyes were perfect ovals, and she had what looked like a small birthmark on the left side other neck. He found that sexy. Her scent was also alluring to him. "You know what, that's my fault." He took her left hand. "You say yo' name Jada, right?"

She nodded. "Yes."

"Well, Jada, I appreciate you for picking me up. It was plenty ma'fuckas that rolled right past me as if I was nothing, and you didn't. I appreciate that. When I get back to my crib, I'ma make sure I hit your hand. How does that sound?"

She pulled her hand away from him. "I didn't do this for money. I did it because it was the right thing to do. A little appreciation and kindness is all that I desire from you. I'll step out so you can use the phone." She walked toward the door.

Stevo couldn't help looking down at her ass as it poked through her skirt. He watched it jiggle like Jell-O. Even in his state of pain he couldn't deny that she was a beautiful woman. "Jada, I don't care what you're saying. I'ma make this up to you. I really do appreciate what you did and are doing for me." His eyes remained glued to her ass the entire time.

She looked over her shoulder at him. "All I ask is for appreciation and kindness. That's it." She eased out of the bedroom and closed the door.

Stevo fell against the bed as soon as she was gone. He pulled himself up and grabbed his phone. He called Sasha. Each second that it took for her to answer, he felt like kicking her ass. When she finally came on the other end he felt like he was going to faint.

"Hello?" Sasha answered.

"Bitch, I need you to get in the car and bring yo monkey ass out here to West Allis. I need a fix. Go into my stash and bring me a zip of my shit. Hurry up!"

"Okay, daddy. Text me the address and the combination to your safe, and I'll be right there."

"Awright." He began to text her the much-needed information. When he finished, he fell to his knees and dropped the phone. He was sick.

***

Makaroni stepped off of the last basement stair and into the darkness. "Montana? Where you at girl?" He could hear the sounds of Ella Mai's *Close* playing out of the speakers that were in the basement. Ella Mai was Montana's favorite singer. He stepped further into the basement waiting for his eyes to adjust.

Montana came from beside the stairs and slid her arms around his waist. She turned him around, and before he could utter a word, she kissed his lips. Her fingers started to undo his Gucci belt. "I don't give a fuck what you talking about Makaroni. This dick belong to me now. You can fuck off with Cassidy from time to time, but ain't nobody about to come in between our bond. I'd rather kill that bitch before I let that happen." She sucked all over his lips. Her hand dipped into his boxers and gripped his dick. She squeezed it and moaned from the thickness of it. She could feel it throbbing in her hand.

Makaroni squeezed her ass cheeks. She had on a short skirt that came to just below her backside. He yanked it up to reveal that she was without panties. His fingers searched her slit from the back. Her sex lips were fully engorged. He played over them.

Montana turned around and rubbed her ass all over his hard piece. She could feel the heat of him along her crease. She moaned with her head tilted backward. Her moan traveled up and through the vent that was positioned right above them. "I need you Makaroni. I been feening for you, big bruh. Ain't you been feening for me, too?" She moved her ass from side to side to manipulate his piece. Her fleshy cheeks felt like hot pillows against his head.

Makaroni groaned. "Hell yeah, Montana. You already know yo lil' ass drive me crazy." He bent her over the washer and kicked her feet apart. "I'm finna fuck this pussy, sis. That's what you want ain't it?"

Montana was so horny for him that she licked the top of the washing machine. Her juices ran down her inner thighs. "Yeah, Mack. Please, fuck me. I need it so bad." She popped her ass back and spaced her feet even more for him.

Maisey sat up in bed and kicked the covers off of her. She swore that she was hearing things. She crawled out of bed and knelt by the vent that led straight up into her bedroom from the basement. She placed her ear to it to hear better.

Makaroni sucked on the back of Montana's neck. He slid his hands under her tank top and squeezed her titties. Her nipples poked up against his palms. He pulled them. "These titties getting so sexy, Montana. Yo lil' ass getting so thick all of a sudden." He groaned. He licked all over her neck and sucked hard on it while his piece rested along her ass crack.

"That's 'cause you been dicking me down. I can't help but to get thick. I love it, bruh. I swear I do."

Makaroni turned her around and sat her on the washer. He opened her thighs wide. Her skirt flipped back into her lap. His face disappeared in between her legs. He sniffed hard. The aroused scent of her pussy drove him insane. He opened her folds and licked up and down them. His tongue flicked the button of her clitoris over and over until her cream was running out of her. Then he slurped it up loudly before trapping her pearl with his lips and flickering his tongue from side to side.

Montana arched her back. She squeezed her titties. "Makaroni! Un. Unn. Unn. Shit. Shit. Shit. Ooo. Shit." She pulled her nipples and came hard when Makaroni slid two fingers deep into her middle.

Makaroni could feel Montana cumming all over his fingers. He pulled them out and sucked them into his mouth. Then his face was back in between her legs licking, and slurping. His nose sniffed up her forbidden scent. He picked her up and slid her down on his dick. Her hot glove enveloped him. She moaned, and bit into his neck. Makaroni manhandled her. He tossed her up and down while he leaned slightly back to give her as much of his dick as he could.

"Mack. Mack. Uhhhh. Big bruh. Uhhhh shit! Unn. Unn. Fuck!" Her eyes rolled into the back of her head. She crossed her arms around his neck. Every time his piece went deep, she felt as if she were ready to cum. He was so wide, and long. "You. Belong. To. Me. Uhhhh. Mack. You. Are. Mine."

"Yeah. Yeah. Shit, sis. Fuck. Uhhhh." Makaroni fell to the ground with her. They landed on top of a dirty pile of clothes. His hips fucked her faster and faster. Her pussy started to make wet slouchy noises. He ripped her tank top down the middle. Her breasts came spilling out. He smushed them together and sucked on the hard tips simultaneously while he slammed into her pelvis.

Montana ran her tongue all over her lips. The feeling of Makaroni reaching depths within her that had never been hit before was overwhelming. He was so hot between her thighs. She pulled him down. She licked his sweaty neck, then bit him again. "Uhhhh! Mack! I love you! I fuckin' love you!" She screamed.

Makaroni growled. He pumped harder and harder while she bit all over him. He could feel her walls sucking at him. Their blended scents wafted into the air. It added to his arousal. She wrapped her thighs around his waist and sat up to kiss his lips. He felt her jerk, and it was too much. He hollered and came deep within her thrusting harder and harder. Montana bit into his neck and screamed her passion.

"Fuck! I love you so much, Mack! I don't wanna share you wit' Cassidy. I want you all to myself." Her teeth scraped at his neck.

Makaroni slowly worked his hips until he was done cumming inside of her. He rolled on to his back and pulled her down. His big hands rubbed all over her ass. "Shorty, this is us. I love you, too."

Montana sat back and looked into his eyes. "You think it can be just us though, Makaroni? Do I really have to share you with her?" She hated herself for feeling so emotional. She knew what he was proposing was nearly impossible. Their relationship was never supposed to have extended to the bedroom, and now that it had it shouldn't have left it. Montana felt hooked. Lost. Connected in a way that wasn't supposed to be designated for Makaroni, yet something in her couldn't let him go. She couldn't leave her feelings in the bedroom.

Makaroni pulled her down. "We'll figure shit out. For now, we better get from down here and shower. Mama catch us, it's a wrap."

It wasn't the answer that Montana was looking for, but she didn't want to poke the bear. It was what it was. "Okay, baby, but just hold me for a minute." She snuggled into him and closed her eyes. For just a second, she reopened them so she could see a hint of his face. She smiled.

Maisey held her hand over her mouth. She was shocked. She couldn't believe what she had just heard and saw. Her babies, under her own roof. The thought was almost enough to give her a heart attack. She rose from her seated position on the basement steps and left both Makaroni and Montana hugged up on the floor. Their scents heavy in the air.

Ghost

Chapter 5

Two weeks after being shot, Stevo found himself inside of a seedy Motel, half naked, and fully hooked on the Rebirth. He sat on the edge of the Motel bed while Sasha laid out sleep. He took an eighth of an ounce of the Rebirth and made ten hefty lines. He rolled up a hundred-dollar bill and took two of the lines hard. While he pinched his nostrils, he swallowed his spit. The high took over him almost immediately. He felt as if he were floating.

Sasha yawned, and stretched her arms over her head. She curled into a ball and opened her eyes. She spotted Stevo with his head bent in front of the Rebirth filled mirror. She got the shivers. She imagined the Rebirth being in her system and started to shake. She crawled over to him. "Daddy, I'm sick. Can I have a taste?"

Stevo picked his head up after taking a line hard and held it backward. Now he felt like he was in Paradise. "Bitch, what have you done today to earn anythang from me?"

Sasha felt like she wanted to cry. Not this again she thought. "I'll do anything you say. You already know that. Please, don't do me like this. All you gotta do is tell me what you need for me to do." She whimpered. "Please, can I have a little taste? I just need enough to get my sick off." She ran her fingers through her nappy curls. Where there was once bounce and sheen to her hair, now it was dry and frizzy. Her scalp was full of dandruff. Her under arms itched. She hadn't showered in a week, and she was okay with it. She crawled under Stevo's arm and tried to kiss his cheek.

He muffed her into the bed. "Bitch, you thank this a ma'fuckin' game? Huh?"

"No."

"You don't get shit free from me. You gon' work for every thang you get." He grabbed a handful of her hair and slung her to the floor. He was disgusted by her, and her neediness. In his mind, her beauty was wavering. He felt that she was on the decline. He had hit her pussy so much that it was old news to him. He needed newer, more fresh pussy.

Sasha felt the stomach pains radiating through her. She curled into the fetal position. Tears poured out of her eyes. "This isn't fair. I need that dope, Stevo. You got me hooked on this shit. You did this to me." She whimpered.

"Bitch, shut up. And what about me, huh? Who did this shit to me? Who gon' feed me when I'm down and out? No muthafuckin' body. That's who!" He tooted another line hard.

Jada hopped out of her Benz truck and pulled her coat tighter around her. She scanned the neighborhood and grew fearful. Everywhere she looked she saw whores pacing up and down the busy street of Lisbon selling their body. Dope Boys were also on the move to sell as many bags as they could. She watched a group of gang bangers walk past the motel. They mugged her and looked her up and down with sexual lust before going on their way. She waited until she could no longer see them and jogged to Stevo's room door. She beat on it four times and stood back.

Stevo slid his hand under his pillow and grabbed his .40 Glock. He cocked it and ran to the side of the door. "Say, man, who the fuck is it?"

Jada took a step back, second-guessing her intentions. *Maybe this wasn't the right time*, she reasoned. She had been without him her entire life. Maybe she didn't need him now. She started to walk away.

"I said who is it?" Stevo felt his adrenalin coursing through him. He felt he was under attack. The old knocking on the door and not answering trick was the oldest kick door move in the world he thought. He refused to fall for it. He thought about climbing out of the bathroom window and running around to the front of the motel to catch the perpetrator off guard. If it even looked like a Jack Boy he was finger fucking his gun. He pulled the silencer out of his pocket and screwed it on. "Bitch, go in the bathroom and don't come out unless I tell you to."

Sasha stood up holding her stomach. She got a few paces and fell to her knees. "Daddy, I'm sick. Please, can I have a taste?"

Stevo pointed at the bathroom. "Go!"

"Okay." She got up and hurried into it now in full on tears.

Stevo slowly unlocked the door and placed his hand on the knob. He held the gun up at the right height of the average male. He took a deep breath and pulled it open. He jumped back.

Jada was about to knock again. When she saw Stevo standing in the doorway shirtless with a gun in his hand, she let out a scream. Then she threw her hands up. "Please, don't shoot."

Stevo grabbed her by the jacket and pulled her inside. He locked the door. "Man, what the fuck are you doing here? Did you bring the cops with you?"

She shook her head. "No. Never. I-I-I." She couldn't get her brain to act right. The gun was spooking her. It brought her back to the terrible times of her childhood.

"Bitch, you what? You done said I like three times." He jacked her up against the door. His crotch smushed her pelvis.

She could smell his sweat. There was a hint of must with left over deodorant that needed to be renewed. His breath was stale, not quite funky, but off putting. "Stevo, is your mother named Cassidy?"

He jacked her up even tighter. "Yeah, bitch, and what about it?"

"Is your father named Seth?"

"That's who Cassidy say it is. Why?"

"Because if those are your parents, then I'm your sister. My name is Jada. They gave me up for adoption when I was only two years old. We have the same mother but different fathers. My father's name is Clarkson."

Stevo released her. He bucked his eyes. "Are you serious?" He was so high that he had to be imagining things.

Jada straightened out her Columbia spring coat. "Yes, I'm serious. Here." She handed him the wallet that he left behind at her place. "I know you might not approve, but I looked you up. Our eyes are too similar. You look just like her. She held up a picture of Cassidy on her phone. The picture was a close up of their mother. "I've been too afraid to approach her. But ever since I ran into you on the street, I felt like it was destiny's way of saying that we need to be a part of each other." She looked past his shoulder and saw the mirror full of Rebirth. She grew solemn. She looked back into his eyes. "Are you angry?"

Stevo stared at her for a long time with the gun in his hand. He was speechless. He grabbed her and wrapped her into his arms. "Man, sis, I hate our mother for what she did to you. I swear to God that I was going to come looking for you. I always felt a need to find you." He held her tight. He kissed the side of her cheek.

Jada was already in tears. "I don't know why she didn't want me. But that's okay. I'm stronger now than I have ever been." She hugged him closer to her body.

Stevo stepped back and wiped her tears away. He looked into her eyes and for the first time in a long time he felt compassion for somebody. His throat grew tight. The sight of her tears seemed to split his heart. "Jada, how about we catch up a lil' bit. I would love to get to know you. What do you say?" Jada nodded. "I would love that." She hugged him again.

***

Makaroni made his rounds throughout the city of Milwaukee. He would take two bricks of the Rebirth and drop them off at his bag houses. There his workers would aluminum foil and bag up the Rebirth before the product was sent to the Trap house on that street that did all of the distribution. After the money was made, his Dope Boy treasurer would pick it up and take the cash to his safe house. Makaroni would then pick up the money four days out of the week always during midnight. He had a smooth operation going. Within a matter of weeks, he'd went from a few traps houses to nearly ten. The Rebirth was taking the city by storm. The addicts were insane over it, and the demand for it was at its highest point.

Two weeks after he'd gotten back from Memphis, Montana pulled up on him with Kandace sitting in the passenger seat. Both ladies were fresh back from getting their hair, fingers and toes done. Montana had bought Kandace a matching skintight Yves St. Laurent skirt dress like her own that had Kandace looking well beyond her years. She tapped the horn twice to get Makaroni's attention. He was just coming out of his stash house with a book bag of the Rebirth containing eight bricks.

Makaroni came to the truck and stuck his head inside of it. Behind him were two bloodthirsty savages that were on security. They watched Makaroni closely and got ready to spray anything that looked out of place. "What's good, Shorty?" He kissed Montana on the forehead.

She winced in agitation. For a second she disliked that Kandace was present. She was due for a kiss on the lips from Makaroni but she had to play it cool. "Nothing. We just getting back from having a lil' girl's day out. I wanted to stop by to make sure you were good. You don't need me to make any runs for you, do you? Have you eaten anything?"

Makaroni laughed. "Don't be acting like mama and shit. I'm good. I got a few drop-offs to make, and then I'ma head back to mom's crib. What you tryna get into tonight?"

Montana had to catch herself. She wanted to say something real nasty that she knew would've exposed their hand. "Uh, you wanna go out and chill? We ain't did that since I been back in town."

"We could, but what about lil' Shorty right there? She going too?" He asked looking Kandace over. He had to admit that she looked good.

"Yeah, tomorrow her birthday. I was gon' take her out tonight and chill, but if you tryna go out then I'll spend all day with her tomorrow. What do you wanna do?" She asked.

Makaroni nodded at Kandace. "What's good, lil' mama?"

Kandace nodded back. She didn't know if she liked Makaroni or not. She didn't know if he was anything like Stevo. They were best friends. She was always told that birds of a feather flocked together.

"Aw, so you don't speak no more?" He asked Kandace.

"I do. I'm good." She looked past him, and then out the other side of the window opposite Makaroni. She wasn't trying to give him the time of the day.

Makaroni picked up on her coldness right away. He felt some type of way. Then it was fuck her as far as he was concerned. "I'll tell you what. I'ma handle dis business, and then I'll hit you up on Facebook. We can go out tonight and kick back. Cool?"

Montana smiled. "Cool."

"Don't forget to tell him about the business side of things." Kandace reminded her.

"Oh yeah, she got a lil' crew of girls that's trying to get they feet wet in the Game." Montana looked up at Makaroni to see his response.

"Get they feet wet doing what?" He wanted to know.

"Hustlin', nigga. Fuck you mean? We gon' hustle. Sell pussy. Whatever else it takes. We trying to get our bands up just like these niggas you got working for you. Only thing is that we are more loyal, and we'll buss that gun quicker than any one of yo niggas would."

Makaroni laughed. "Girl, please. What you know about bussing a gun?"

Kandace slid a .45 out of her Fendi bag. "Nigga, don't get shit twisted because I got a pussy between my legs. My ma'fuckin' balls are invisible, but they are there. Fuck wit' it if you want to."

Makaroni frowned and looked Montana over. "Is she serious?"

"She hit up Stevo punk ass multiple times. I'm fuckin wit' Kandace the long way. I owe her for what she did to that nigga. Straight up. Far as that hustling shit go, what do you have to lose? She already got her ducks in a row. It's like ten lil' bad ass girls that's down to roll under her. I trust her to run her lil' clique with an iron fist. All we gotta do is give her a chance. Money ain't got no gender. Never forget that. Besides that trapping shit, I got a few more ideas that I wanna run by you."

Makaroni stepped away from the Montana's truck and placed his hand under his shirt. He clutched the handle of his .44 and eyed a Jeep that had tinted windows. It stopped on the corner of their street and remained still. Makaroni looked over his shoulder to make sure his Hittas were on point. "Y'all see this shit?" They answered him by upping their weapons and cocking them.

Montana rubber-necked to see what they were looking at. "Mack, what's wrong?" She asked looking him over.

"Montana, we gon' get together later. Gon' 'head and pull off." He ordered.

"What's the matter?" She became worried.

"Man, pull off, sis. Damn. Hurry up."

"Okay. You ain't gotta holler." Montana threw her truck in drive and pulled away from the curb reluctantly.

As she was pulling away, a Jeep came speeding down the street. Makaroni backed away from the curb. It zipped past his Trap and sped up until it was behind Montana's truck. Montana was halted at a stop sign. Two Shooters jumped out of the back of the Jeep with handguns, and ski masks covered their faces. They rushed Montana's truck, bussing back to back. *Bocka! Bocka! Bocka! Bocka!*

Makaroni took off running as fast as he could toward the shootout with his heart beating like crazy inside of his chest. He imagined the shooters killing his sister, and it was enough to make him want to pass out. He forced himself to run faster with his gun in his hand.

Montana ducked after her back window exploded. She fell to the floor of her truck screaming. "What the fuck is going on? Help!"

Kandace crawled toward the back of the Jeep. She waited until there was a break in the shooting. She jumped up bussing her Glock. *Boom. Boom. Boom. Boom.* Her bullets

52

punched holes in the windshield of the Jeep, shattering it. The Shooters ran back to the Jeep and jumped inside. The Jeep sped backwards, sending smoke from its tires.

Makaroni met it halfway. He ran into the middle of the street bussing. *Bocka! Bocka! Bocka! Bocka!* The Jeep sped past him and made a backwards U-turn. Makaroni's shooters chopped at the Jeep's body with their assault rifles. The Jeep rocked with bullets tinking off of it. The Shooters ducked inside of the Jeep as the barrage of bullets chopped away at the exterior of their getaway truck. The driver stepped on the gas and skirted off of the street. All around, people were hidden behind cars. Some snuck under parked cars or ran into their houses to escape the gun war.

Makaroni yanked open Montana's door and pulled her out. He looked into her face. "Are you okay?"

She nodded. She was shaking as if she were freezing cold. She hugged him. "Who was that, Mack?"

Makaroni shook his head. "I don't know. But me and my niggas gon' most definitely find out."

Kandace stood in the middle of the street with a gun in her hand. "Whoever it was, them niggas was a bunch of cowards. How the fuck you couldn't kill two females that you caught off guard? Pussy niggas." She spit on the concrete and wiped her mouth with the back of her hand. "Come on, Montana, let's get the fuck out of here."

Makaroni held Montana protectively. He couldn't help but to eye Kandace. She had heart. He liked that. "Say, Shorty?"

Kandace nodded. "Whut up?"

"You remember that shit you asked me about? You know, trapping and all of that shit?" He asked.

"Yeah, what about it?"

"I'ma fuck wit' you. Let me clean up this mess first. Get yo ducks in a row, and I'm most certainly gon' fuck wit' you."

She wiped her mouth again. "You just came up, Play-boy." She eased into Montana's passenger's seat after wiping the glass from it.

Chapter 6

It was a dark and breezy night. Two days after Rubio Flores had given JaMichael a two-week extension to get things figured out within the city of Memphis. JaMichael had two weeks to annihilate Phoenix, or Rubio promised to step in and take care of them. Then Rubio's Cartel would become the sole possessors and distributors of the Rebirth. JaMichael refused to let that happen, and so did Phoenix. DaBaby tightened his leather gloves and made sure that his fingers were as deep into them as they could go. He took the glass cutter out of his inside coat pocket and placed it on the patio window to Phoenix's home. Behind him, the clear blue waters to the swimming pool sparkled and shimmered in the moonlight. Loud music played inside of the house, indicating that somebody had to be home. That brought a sadistic smile to his face. He clamped the glass cutter on to the window. Then he locked it in place. He turned it counterclockwise until a circular hole appeared. He pulled the glass cutter backward and removed the glass.

Roscoe stepped forward and slid his hand into the hole. He searched for a lock until he found one. He clicked it open. He nodded at DaBaby and took his .9 millimeter out of his waistband.

DaBaby slowly opened the door and stepped into the first room. His black boots sunk into the soft white carpet. He could hear a bunch of laughing coming from the other room. He waved for Roscoe to follow him. He crept across the carpet, and made haste down the hallway, where it turned into a big den. There sitting on the couch were April, Phoenix's wife, and four of her girlfriends. They were having a book club meeting.

Roscoe ran directly from the dark hallway into the den. He spotted April right away. All five women screamed. He grabbed April by the throat, picked her up into the air and slammed her to the ground so hard that she bounced off of it and was knocked out cold.

"Awright, bitches, y'all lay it down. Everybody on their stomachs right now. Move!" DaBaby ordered.

Roscoe knelt and smacked April as hard as he could. Her yellow face was the color of red. "Wake up. Where is Phoenix? Bitch, don't say you don't know either."

April was dizzy. She felt like she had been in a car accident again. She blinked repeatedly and hoped that she was in a nightmare. "What?"

Smack! Smack! Smack! Roscoe swung as hard as he could, slapping the dog shit out of her. "Where the fuck is Phoenix?" He pulled her up by her dress top. "If I have to ask you one more muthafuckin' time, I swear to God I'ma—" *Boom!* Roscoe's head exploded. He flew backward against the wall and fell to his knees with brain matter leaking out of his cranium. He wound up on his side, lifeless.

"Bitch ass nigga, here I go!" Phoenix hollered. He jumped over the banister of the stairs, shooting at a retreating DaBaby. *Boom! Boom! Boom! Boom*! "April, stay down!" *Boom!*

Blocka! Blocka! Blocka! DaBaby bussed back and took off running down the hallway. He jumped and crashed through the patio glass. Making a boisterous retreat, he ran as fast as he could across the lawn and hopped the fence.

Phoenix got outside and looked both ways. He heard rustling in the bushes and took off running in the direction of DaBaby. He hopped the fence and tailed him, making up ground with each stride of his long legs.

DaBaby's chest was tight. He looked over his shoulders to see if he was being trailed. When he was sure that he wasn't he slowed his pace. He jogged to the stolen Chevy Caprice and started it up. He kept seeing the image of Roscoe's head exploding. He couldn't believe that he had lost his homey to the gun. He pulled away.

Phoenix jumped out of the bushes and on to the top of the hood of the car. He aimed at DaBaby through the windshield. *Bocka! Bocka! Bocka*! Three holes appeared in the glass.

DaBaby felt the slugs enter into his vest, zip through it and pierce his skin. The heat seared him. He hollered out in pain. He bussed up at Phoenix. *Boom! Boom! Boom! Boom!*

Phoenix jumped off of the cars and ran around to the side of the Chevy. He fired through the glass, shattering it. "Duffel Bag, nigga! Fuck you thought this was?" *Boom! Boom!*

Both of the final slugs punched into Dababy's shoulder. He stepped on the gas and stormed away from a shooting Phoenix, with blood all over him. "That bitch ass nigga! That bitch ass Phoenix. I'ma get that nigga. Watch!" He hollered out loud.

***

Stevo slipped next to Jada on the couch and placed his arm around her shoulders. Ever since he'd found out that she was his sister, he hadn't let her out of his sights. It was days later since the revelation, and he still couldn't believe it. He pulled her closer to him on her couch. "Man, sis, it feel so good knowing that I finally got some family now."

She smacked her lips and poked over at him. "Boy, are you serious? You are the one that grew up with the family. I was bounced around from foster home to foster home. Most of the homes I landed in were full of perverted men with one thing on their mind. It's amazing that after so many years, right before I aged out, I found the right family. Now I'm in medical school, and I'm set to be somebody that I can be proud of."

He kissed her forehead. "Well, that's all good. I'm proud of you." He grabbed the bowl of popcorn off of the table. "So, what movie we finna watch?" Stevo didn't really care what he watched as long as he could be under her.

"This is the last Star Wars movie. They say they aren't making anymore, and I gotta see this. I had way too many exams to see it when it came out in the theaters. But I gotta see it now. I think it's kind of cool that I get to watch it with my brother though."

Stevo blushed. "Yeah, I guess it is. Well gon' 'head and start it. I'll be right back." The Rebirth was calling him. He needed to boost his high.

"Awright, well, don't be too long. You sure you don't want me to pause it?"

He waved her off. "N'all, I ain't gon' miss nothin' but the previews. It's all good. The bathroom the second door from the left right?"

"Right." She folded her legs under her and prepared to watch a bunch of previews that was sure to encourage her to download more movies.

"Cool." As Stevo was making his way down the hallway there was a knock at the door. He stopped and looked back toward Jada. She got up and headed for the front door. He was about to be nosey when a sharp pain shot through his stomach, nearly doubling him over. He took a deep breath, hurried inside of the bathroom, closed the door and locked it. He sat on the covered toilet and pulled the Rebirth out of his pocket. He dumped a nice portion on the ledge of the sink and snorted it hard. The Rebirth took effect immediately. Euphoria shot all over his brain. He took another line straight to the dome and moaned out loud. When he got back into the living room, he was met with the sight of a red-haired white man his height and build with his arm around Jada.

Jada laughed at a corny joke the man cracked, and spotted Stevo coming out of the hallway. "Oh, good. Stevo, this is Barron. Barron, this is Stevo. He's the brother I was telling you that I recently discovered."

Barron took his arm from around Jada's neck and extended his hand to Stevo. "Nice to meet you, Stevo."

Stevo looked at his hand as if it were lathered in feces. He scanned him over quickly and decided he could break his neck on the first try if he had to. He stepped past him. "What is he doing here? I thought you and I were working on getting to know each other?"

Jada looked disgruntled. She ran her fingers through her well permed hair. "Hey, it's a big television. Seventy inches. Barron goes to the University of Minnesota. I barely get to see him. I forgot that he was dropping in this weekend."

Barron got a bad vibe from Stevo right away. Something told him to get out of there, and he was dead set on listening to it. "Hey, Jada, it's cool. I'll catch you at another time." He grabbed his jacket off of the sofa.

"Barron, wait. You don't have to go. We were just going to watch a movie together. Stevo, tell him he doesn't have to go." She'd been missing Barron. She missed being held by him. She missed their conversations. Barron had been her boyfriend for three years, and she loved him. In addition to all of this, her lady parts were crying out for some loving. Intense studying, and the long drive between Wisconsin and Minnesota meant that on most nights she had to please herself or go without. She wasn't the cheating type. Barron moved closer to the door. "Please, tell him, Stevo, that he doesn't have to leave." She turned to her brother, pleading.

"Man, I don't know dude to be telling him shit. I don't wanna spend no time with him. I came here to spend some quality time with you. Fuck Barron." Stevo spat.

"I think I've heard enough." He held his hands up and opened the door. He stepped out of it and slammed it behind himself.

"Barron, wait!" Jada called. She ran to the door. But it was too late. Barron hopped into his Corvette and sped away from the curb with his wheels screeching.

Jada stood with her back to the door. She covered her face with both hands. She was pissed. She took her hands away and found Stevo. "You had no right to behave like that. You can't just drop into my life, trying to take over. You don't own me, Stevo. Now that was very rude. We are going to hit Barron up, and you are going to apologize to him. Do I make myself clear?"

"Bitch, you crazy. The day I apologize to any ma'fucka I don't know is the same day they end world hunger." He laughed. "It's like I said before. I came over to see and spend time with you, not him. I don't care how he's feeling. He gotta deal with that on his own, and if you feeling some type of way then so be it."

Jada was stunned. She glared at him with her temper rising. "Are you fuckin' serious right now?" She took two steps toward him.

"Dead ass serious." Stevo returned her stare. He felt himself getting annoyed.

For as long as she had been in his life, he'd felt nothing but love and admiration for her. But all of that was quickly fading away as his true self was emerging to the forefront. Jada stood looking at him for a few more moments. She began to shake her head in utter disbelief. "You know what,

Stevo? I think it's time you leave. You have overstayed your welcome." She unlocked the front door, pulling it open.

Stevo remained still. "Yo, you finna shit on me for that redheaded nigga that just walked up out of here? For real? Yo' own mafuckin' brother?"

"I'm sorry things didn't work out the way we expected them to. It seems we didn't connect as much as we thought we would." Jada was ready for him to go. She didn't like his aura. She felt the bad vibes beaming off him. She wanted him out of her house as soon as possible.

Stevo's temper went from zero to a hundred real quick. He put a fake smile on his face. There was no way he was willing to lose the sister that he'd just found after so many years of wondering who she was. He thought about the quantity of Rebirth that he had inside of his coat pocket, along with the few syringes that he had used to hook the females that Sasha brought home to replace Carmen and Kandace. Two girls so far, he had yet to learn their names. "You know what, Jada? We gon' play things your way." He grabbed his coat off the coat rack and slid it onto his shoulders. "I really am sorry for coming at your boyfriend like that. I guess I just really wanted this night to be special for us. I looked forward to watching a movie with my sister. It's crazy, I know. But it's all good though." He stepped up to the door. "Can I at least have a hug from my baby sister before I go?"

Jada felt horrible. She felt like she might've been over-reacting just a bit. "Hey, Stevo, maybe we just need a few days apart. We'll get our heads together, and then we'll re-connect, and watch that movie together. How does that sound?"

Stevo nodded. "Sounds like a plan. Come here." He held his arms open for her to walk into them.

Jada relented. She closed the door and slowly walked toward him. "You still have to go though. I think I'm going to get me some sleep." She stepped into his arms.

Stevo hugged her close. He kissed her soft cheek and inhaled her fragrant scent. He smiled for a few seconds. When he felt her trying to pull back, his smile turned into a frown. He slipped from Jada and wound up behind her. He placed her in a sleeper hold.

She smacked at his arm. "Let me go!" She muffled, scratching at his huge bicep.

Stevo tightened his grip, applying a serious amount of pressure. "You are my sister. Mine! Fuck that dude! You supposed to care about me more than him. Me; only me." He was squeezing so hard that he was shaking.

Jada smacked at his arm. She grew faint. She clawed at him. Her knees went weak. Her eyes crossed, and then she was out like a light switch.

Stevo laid her down and knelt beside her. He pulled out one of the syringes. He went through the whole process of getting the Rebirth ready for injection. He drew up the potent liquid and yanked Jada's arm to him. Once he had it pulled out the long way, he found her thickest vein and injected the Rebirth into her system. She smiled and moaned. Stevo threw it away. He grabbed her left one and found another thick vein. He drew up more of the Rebirth, following the same process as before, injecting her again. He wanted Jada addicted. Fully dependent on *him*. He couldn't lose her again. He felt that she was the only real family he had. He hated his parents for giving his sister away. He hated his father for being so weak.

Jada shook on the ground as the drug traveled through her system. She smacked her lips together. High levels of serotonin shot through her brain. She felt happy and numb.

Her eyelids fluttered. She frowned and suddenly felt cold. Her teeth chattered. The Rebirth had dropped her blood sugar considerably low.

Stevo picked her up. He carried her to the door and locked it. A minute later, he laid her down in her bed. He stripped her down to her bra and panties, pulling the covers over her body. He laid beside her. "I love you, sis. I don't know what you used to, but you belong to me now. Mafuckas been taking shit from me my whole life. But they ain't gon' have the chance to take you away. Fuck that. I ain't even finna let you take yourself away from me. You hear me, bitch?" He grabbed her around the throat. Jada kicked her legs wildly. He released her then laid beside her, hugging her to his chest. "We will never part again. Never!" He meant exactly that.

Ghost

Chapter 7

It was a warm and sunny Thursday afternoon, a day after Makaroni and Montana had lost themselves in the throes of passion inside of Maisey's basement. Makaroni strolled into the house with a bag full of KFC, and his arm around Montana's neck. They thought it would be cool to surprise their mother with lunch since it was her second consecutive day off of work. Montana took the bags out of Makaroni's hand and kissed him on the cheek. She peered into his eyes and gave him a knowing look that said she yearned for him.

"Shorty, you betta chill yo ass out. Remember we gotta be cool. Mama ain't no damn fool." He whispered, looking down the hallway toward Maisey's bedroom.

"Boy, ain't nobody thinking 'bout you. I'm ready to eat." She smiled devilishly, taking a step toward him, planting a kiss on the corner of his mouth, leaving a mark from her pink lipstick.

Makaroni heard Maisey's door open. He pushed Montana back, and dusted off his clothes. When Maisey entered the dining room, he was pulling out the chicken boxes, and setting it around the table. "Hey, mama. How are you doing, my Queen?"

Montana walked up and kissed her mother on the cheek. Once again, leaving behind a pink lipstick mark. "Hey, mama."

Maisey didn't know how to feel at seeing her children. Every time she blinked, she saw images of the pair on the floor writhing in sin. She closed her eyes tight and took a deep breath. "I'm fine. How are you two?"

Makaroni stepped up to her to kiss her on the cheek. Maisey saw the pink lipstick on the corner of his mouth. Her eyes went to Montana's lips. Before she knew what she was doing, she swung as fast and as hard as she could and punched Makaroni right on the lipstick. *Pow!* Her knuckles cracked into his mouth and dropped him to the floor. She closed the distance between her and a shocked Montana. She slapped fire from her twice and threw her to the floor. "What the fuck is wrong with the both you? Have y'all lost y'all fuckin' minds?" She snapped.

Makaroni jumped to his feet fuming. He mugged his mother with mounting anger. "Mama, why you hit me?"

Montana was dizzy. It took her a while to get to her feet. When she got there, she staggered a bit. She bounced into the wall and laid against it to gather herself. Her head was spinning.

"Y'all think I'm really stupid, huh? Do ya?"

Makaroni was heated now. "Man, what are you talking about?" He didn't have the slightest idea. He thought that maybe she was still caught up on the mess with Cassidy. If not Cassidy, then maybe his dealings with JaMichael and Jahliya down south.

Maisey pointed at him. "I watched *you* fucking *her* in my basement. You put your fucking penis inside of my daughter. And you." She turned toward Montana, "Bitch, you was making all kinds of noises like it was the best night of your life. When did this sick shit start?" She mugged Montana.

Montana lowered her head. "Mama, I don't know what you're talking about." She lied. "You must've been seeing things."

Maisey cocked her fist back. "Bitch, I'll beat you until every bone in your body is broken. How dare you play me for a fool?"

Montana held up her hands and stepped behind Makaroni. "She tripping."

Maisey stepped into Makaroni's face. "You wanna lie to me, too?"

Makaroni held his silence for a few seconds. He didn't know what to say. He had never lied to his mother before, and he didn't see himself starting any time soon. "N'all, you already know I'ma keep things real with you at all times. That's the way it's always been, and it ain't finna change. But I'ma need you to keep your hands to yourself though." He sucked blood from the split in his lip.

Maisey backed up. "Cool. All I wanna know is how this started."

He nodded. "Mama, me and Montana being playing around with each other since we were curious kids. I don't really know how it started."

"Wrestling." Montana interrupted.

"What?" Maisey asked.

"Wrestling. Makaroni and I used to wrestle when we were little, and for some reason he would always wind up between my legs. I liked how he felt there. As we got older, we horse played, wearing less and less until we wound up doing what you caught us doing." Montana felt relieved that she had finally admitted to her mother the secret she and her brother had kept under wraps for so long. It was out in the open. Now there was nothing to hide. She was no longer worried about the consequences. Both she and Makaroni were grown. There was nothing that Maisey could do about what they were doing.

"Look, mama, I apologize. By me being the oldest, I should've been better. I should've nipped it in the bud but I didn't." Makaroni felt Maisey's disappointed eyes staring him down. He hated disappointing his mother more than anything else in the world.

"So, now what? When are you two going to stop this sick shit? When will y'all stop acting like Satan's children, and do what the fuck y'all are supposed to be doing the right way? With other people, not each-fuckin'-other!" She was so mad that she was shaking.

"I ain't finna mess with nobody if it ain't him. I love Makaroni, and he love me. You just gon' have to deal with it." Montana spoke with more confidence than she actually had.

Maisey took off her earrings and slammed them on the table. "Bitch, when I get through with yo ass you'll never think about sleeping with him again." She rolled back her sleeves and launched at Montana.

Makaroni got in the middle. "Mama, chill. She's just saying that to get to you. We finna fall back from all of that. You got my word." He pushed her all the way back into the hallway and held her.

"Let me go, Makaroni! Get your fuckin' hands off of me." She pushed him so hard that he went stumbling backward. She ran at Montana.

Montana held her guards up. She never thought that she would have to raise a hand against her mother, but she refused to allow for her to beat her senseless. She waited for Maisey to get close enough before she grabbed her and fell to the floor with her. "Mama, chill out. You're tripping over nothing. Please calm down."

Maisey tussled. "Bitch, get off of me. I ain't calming down shit. Y'all ain't finna continue that cycle. Our family is fucked up because of that same shit y'all was doing on that basement floor. If I gotta kill both of my kids to bring an end to it then I will, so help me God." She bucked her hips and threw Montana off of her. She straddled her with one quick move and slapped her across the face, busting her nose.

Makaroni pulled Maisey from Montana. He picked her up in the air and carried her to her bedroom where he dropped her on the bed. "Calm down. Right now!" He roared.

Maisey hopped up and got into his face. "What you say to me, lil' boy?"

"I'm a grown man, mama. Let's get that straight, first and foremost. Secondly, I love you, but you ain't finna be putting yo hands on my sister. Ain't nobody gon' do that, just like I ain't finna let nobody put they hands on you. You need to fall back."

Maisey balled her hands into fists. "Boy, if you don't get yo black ass out of my way, I'm finna break you down to size. I'm not playing either." She sidestepped and pulled a wooden Louisville Slugger bat out of her closet. It still had traces of Seth's blood on it.

Makaroni stood his ground. "We ain't kids no more, mama. Now I gave you my word that it wasn't goin' to happen again. That's the best I can do."

Maisey raised the bat over her head for a second, and then lowered it. She couldn't bring herself to hurt her son like she had Seth. She loved him too much. "Makaroni, you don't understand the cycle, son. All the shit I went through as a kid. All of the sins that have been created because of the same things you two are doing. My God, there is so much that you two don't know. That has to stop. Please, baby. Promise me that it will."

Makaroni pulled her into his embrace. "You ain't told us what's good, mama. How are we supposed to know if you don't tell us anything?"

Maisey held him. "How could I, baby? How could I expose our family's history without admitting the things I have done? Some of the things are the reasons your father isn't here with me today." She dug her face into his chest.

Makaroni held her. He was confused and a bit curious. His whole life he'd been under the impression that his father, Howard, left their family behind to fend for themselves because he was a coward. He thought the responsibly of caring for a woman and his own two kids became too much of a task for his father, so the man split. He ran off to the suburbs and reinvented himself with a white woman and created what he deemed was the perfect family. In doing so, he'd left a young Makaroni and Montana behind along with Maisey. They were forced to fend for themselves in the grimy trenches of Chicago, Illinois and Milwaukee, Wisconsin where the streets were unforgiving and cold. It was one of the reasons Makaroni went so hard to succeed in the Game. He wanted to show Howard that their family didn't need him. That the family he'd left them behind for wasn't the perfect family, but the one with him, Montana and Maisey was the best family. Makaroni took his father's departure personal every single day. He snuck thousands of dollars into his mother's purse at a time to make sure she'd never need for anything. He intercepted the landlord and paid her rent, and other bills online. He never wanted Maisey to feel any less than a Queen. Montana either. He kept his sister closer. Sometimes more close than necessary, but he felt like only God could judge them.

Maisey took a step back and looked into his dark, handsome face. "Baby, are you upset with me? You've been quiet for a while."

"Never, mama. You're my Queen. All I ask is that one day you sit me down and you open your heart to me. I want to know what's going on inside of there." He touched the middle of her chest. "I deserve that."

She nodded. "Yes, baby, you do. And I promise that when I feel the time is right, you will get all of it." She sighed. "Can you give me a little time?"

He pulled her to him and rested his lips against her forehead. "Of course, I can. Take all the time that you need. I love you, my Queen."

Maisey closed her eyes. "I love you too, baby. Please, stay away from Montana. You can love her without making love to her. Do you hear me?"

"I do." His phone buzzed with Stevo's picture flashing on it.

Stevo: Bruh, we need to meet up. Meet me at Washington Park tonight at nine O'Clock. Important.

"What's the matter, baby?"

"Nothin', I gotta go do somethin'. I'll catch you later, mama." He kissed her forehead again and stepped out of her room, closing the door behind him. When he got outside, Montana was already sitting in his truck. He got in. "What you doing in here?"

"Mack, I don't know what she told you in there, but we are in too deep. I love you with all of my heart, just like you love me. I'm not finna listen to nobody trying to tell me how to love you. I love mama, but we are grown. This is mine." She reached into his lap and grabbed his pipe possessively. It felt like a pole in her hand. "I'm not playing about you."

Makaroni felt a sudden urge of possession. He looked into Montana's eyes. "I feel the same way, sis. It's some shit going on that mama wanna let me know about in her own time. Until she do, we are who we are. I can't get enough of yo ass either."

Montana melted. She was prepared for a big fight between the two of them. She felt relieved. "Cool then. So, I'll see you later on tonight?"

"Yeah, I got some shit I gotta handle right now, but we'll link up later. I love you."

Montana looked back at Maisey's house, searching for a sight of her in the window. She threw caution to the wind and grabbed Makaroni, planting a quick kiss on his lips. "Be safe out here, bruh. I'll see you later."

Chapter 8

Jada opened her eyes to find Stevo standing over her with a big smile on his face. Sweat slid down the sides of his face. He was shirtless, and wet. The room felt muggy, and hot. She tried to pull the covers back, but they were stuck to her. She sat up with a pounding headache. She wanted to puke. "What's happening right now? Why is it so hot in here, Stevo?"

"Girl, you need this heat. This heat is going to help the Rebirth sink all into yo' system the right way." He held a syringe in his hand, and up for her to see it.

Jada focused and frowned. She threw the covers off of her body. She was nude underneath. She could smell herself. Her deodorant had worn off a few hours ago. "What the hell are you holding?" She felt a sharp pain shoot through her stomach. She grabbed her abdomen and hunched over.

"This is the shit that's gon' help you get rid of those stomach pains." Stevo sat on the bed beside her. He could smell her funk from the heat. He loved it. The sweat allowed for her pores to regurgitate the Rebirth through them. The scent of the drug wafted into the air.

"What is it though?" She had a migraine that made it nearly impossible to open her eyelids all the way. Her mouth was dry. Her inner forearms itched, and she suddenly felt like passing gas but feared what would come out, so she held it.

"This is the magic medicine that's going to keep you and I together forever. You're my ma'fuckin' sister and I ain't finna lose you no more. I need you in my life. That's how I feel."

Another sharp pain shot through her abdomen. She curled into a fetal position with her knees nearly to her chest. "I feel horrible, Stevo. What have you done to me?"

Stevo looked her over. He felt a twinge of remorse for Jada. After all, she was his little sister. He didn't want to hurt her. He only wanted her to listen to him, and for her to choose him over anybody else. "Look, Jada, you need some more of this. As soon as you take a small dosage of this, you'll feel all better for two straight hours. Then we'll have to hit you again."

Jada's stomach rumbled. She squeezed into a tighter ball. Her mouth went from dry to salivating. "What is that shit, Stevo? It's killing me."

"Bitch, I already told you. It's the drug that's gon' keep you and I together forever. Now give me your arm." He tried to grab her.

Jada pushed him off. She hopped out of the bed and found a corner of the room. "You're not putting that shit into my body anymore. I don't know what it is, and it's not right. Please, just leave my house, Stevo. I don't want anything else to do with you. I hate that I even stopped for you!" She hollered.

Stevo felt the emotional slug, and it pissed him off. He stood up seething. "You know what? I'm done asking you to follow my commands. Bitch, you finna listen to me. Now get yo ass over here."

Jada backed up. She scanned the room for something that could be used as a weapon. She settled on the lamp that was on the side of her bed. She eased closer to it. "Stevo, you need to calm down. There is no way that you can be angry with me for not wanting you to pump my system full of that— awwwww!" She fell to the floor holding her stomach.

Stevo rushed her and pushed her on to her back. "Gimme your arm. I don't wanna see you hurting like this. You're my baby sister. I love you, Jada. I swear to God, I love you so much. Just give me your arm. Sasha! Sasha! Bitch, get yo yellow ass in here!" He called. Stevo invited Sasha over to bring more of the Rebirth and to help him break Jada in.

"Get off of me, Stevo! Please. I'm sick. I need to take a cold shower. Please get off of me!" Jada wailed.

Sasha rushed into the room high off of the Rebirth. Her eyes were low. Her senses were thrown off. She found the pair and dropped beside Stevo. Jada kicked wildly exposing her privates. Sasha hoped that she wasn't about to help him sex her. She didn't mind, but she felt like he didn't need to fuck Jada when he had her. "What do you want me to do, Daddy?"

"Hold my sister arm. The right one, right here." He ordered.

Sasha grabbed Jada's wrist, and pulled. She placed her knee on top of it and rested all of her weight on top of it. "I got her, Daddy."

Stevo took the cap off of the syringe full of Rebirth. He licked Jada's arm, and slid the needle into her vein. He pushed down on the feeder and pulled it out just a tad to draw up his sister's blood. Then he injected it the entire way while she screamed and kicked.

As the Rebirth entered into her system, Jada became quiet. Her eyes rolled into the back of her head. Her clit poked from between her sex lips. She opened her legs wider and came, moaning. Her tongue roamed all over her lips.

Stevo stood up with his arm around Sasha. "Thank you, Shorty."

"You're welcome, Daddy." She kissed him on the cheek. She looked down at Jada. Her thighs were wide open. Her hand played over her pussy. Sasha had been there before. The Rebirth attacked a person's sexual organs hard. It made you feel like you were having the best sex in the world even when you weren't. She smiled and looked up to Stevo. "Daddy, can I have a taste of you? Seeing her making me feel some type of way."

Stevo's dick was rock hard. He wanted to take his eyes off of a writhing Jada, but he couldn't. She stared up at him longingly. He could only imagine what she was feeling. He needed to get the sexual urges out of his system before he did some things he'd regret. He watched Jada slide two fingers into herself and work them. His dick became hard. "Sasha, suck me up lil' mama."

"Stevo, I need you. Please. I need you right here." Jada rubbed the entrance to her pussy. It was soaking wet. Her juices leaked out of her middle and into the crack of her cheeks. Her sex lips were so engorged that they were a shade of red.

"Sasha, hurry up, bitch."

Sasha knelt before him and pulled his piece out. She stroked it for a minute. "I got you, daddy."

Stevo ignored her. As much as he hated to admit it, his eyes were between Jada's thighs. He had never seen a pussy so fat. He wanted to blow his own head off for having those thoughts as he looked down on her. She started to finger herself at full speed. Sasha sucked him into her mouth and went to work just like he'd taught her. Stevo humped into her tight lips, all the while hating himself for imagining that he was fucking Jada, but the Rebirth had taken over him. He eyed Jada's hard nipples that covered majority of her C cup mounds. His eyes trailed down her dark brown stomach, back to her box. She opened it for him. He saw her pink and came inside of Sasha's mouth. He grabbed her head and forced her to take him while he came.

Sasha gagged, and swallowed his seed. She choked and groaned. She had never felt him cum so much. He pushed her off of him. She fell onto her butt. She looked up to him puzzled. He never took his eyes away from Jada. "Daddy, what do you want me to do?"

"Get out of the room. I need to talk to her!" He hollered.

"But, daddy?" Sasha stood up. She mugged Jada who was laying on her back. Her thick thighs were splayed wide. Her gash wide open, and drooling. "I thought you needed me."

"Get the fuck out Sasha, and close the door." He turned to her. "I ain't gon' tell you again."

She felt defeated. She felt worthless. It seemed that every time she felt that she was gaining any ground with Stevo, it was always stripped from under her. She hated that. He was starting to remind her of her selfish father. The man only called on her when he wanted something for himself. He had never taken the time to cater to her needs and emotions. He was self-centered and pretentious. When Sasha first became a part of Stevo's stable he had given her so much attention that for once in her life she felt special. The short term displays of love had captivated her. But now she felt as if it what they had was all dwindling away. Her heart was coming apart at the seams. She eased out of the door and closed it.

Stevo took a step back and locked it. He stepped over to Jada and knelt to her. "You okay?"

Jada was two fingers deep. She pulled them out and held them out to him. "Smell me, Stevo."

Stevo began to shake. "Girl, you tripping. You're my baby sis, I don't get down like th—"

She wiped her juices on his nose and lips. "Smell it."

Stevo humped on top of her and sat up. He could smell her odor heavy now. It appealed to the animal in him. His shaking became worse. His dick was rock hard. Jada wrapped her thighs around him. "What the fuck is wrong wit' you?" He snapped.

Her pussy was on fire. She wanted him. She didn't care who he was. She needed the fire between her thighs to be extinguished. "Fuck me, Stevo. If you don't, then Barron will." She knew that would piss him off.

Stevo grew irate quickly. "Fuck, Barron. Don't you ever say his punk ass name to me again. Do you hear me?"

"Shut up and touch me! Touch me between my legs. Please. Touch me or get the fuck off of me. I'll have anybody do it, but you." She opened her thighs and arched her back. The Rebirth had her clit throbbing like never before. It was so bad that it was driving her crazy. She wanted to scream. "Touch me!" She grabbed his hand and put it between her thighs.

Stevo rested his fingers on her puffy sex lips. They felt hot, and slithery. He trailed them slightly to the right. His fingers slipped into her box. The felt like they had eased into the mouth of a tight Volcano opening. As soon as they sunk into her, she screamed and came all over him. He pulled his hand back. Unsure. This wasn't what he wanted. He just needed for her to stay. For her to not want to leave and abandon him. Sex had been the furthest thing from his brain. Jada humped into the air and yearned for him to touch her. He saw the longing in her eyes. It softened him. "Jada, we can't. That shit ain't cool, sis."

"Please. I need you." She sat up and tried to pull him down to her.

Stevo drew backward. He stood up. His piece jumped. "N'all, man. This ain't what I want from you. I'm not finna

treat you like every other bitch in my life. I love yo lil' ass."
Her grabbed a handful of her hair and pulled her up. He then
tossed her on the bed.

She landed with her thighs wide open. Her hand went
between them again. She was making it so hard for him to
resist her. His morals fought against the demon that was the
Rebirth. Jada crawled across the bed toward him. Her ass in
the air. Her breasts bounced. She got to him and stood on her
knees. "If you don't want me like this, then what do you
want?" She cupped her breasts. The Rebirth was taking over
her common sense. Her sex parts were screaming for attention. She trailed her hand down her stomach, and into her
garden. "Tell me, Stevo, because I can see how hard you are
right now. You want me. Don't you?" She grabbed his naked
pipe and squeezed. Within seconds she was stroking him.

The Rebirth took over Stevo. He closed his eyes and allowed for her to manipulate him. It felt so good to him. So
good, yet so wrong. He opened his eyes just in time to see
her guiding her mouth to his dick. He pushed her back and
tucked his pole into his boxers. "N'all, we ain't finna get
down like that. I love you, girl. You on fire. I got you." He
picked her up and threw her into the middle of the bed.
Opened her thighs and put two fingers into her hole. He figured he had already crossed the line anyway. He rolled his
thumb around her clitoris, while his fingers penetrated her at
full speed. "Come on. Cum for me. This what you wanted,
right? Right?" He increased his speeds.

Jada bucked upward. She opened her mouth wide,
breathing hard. "Unn. Unn. Unn. Yes. Yes. Fuck yes!" Stevo
pinched her clit, sending erotic chills all over her body. He
blew on her lips, and finger fucked her as fast as he could.
Jada closed her eye tightly and came hard. She screamed as
the Rebirth fully took over her. She threw her legs wide open

and laid out, allowing for Stevo to manipulate her however he saw fit. After she came for the third time, she sat up and stuck her hand into his boxer hole. "Fuck me. Now! Now, Stevo!" The more she came, the more her arousal elevated. The Rebirth was created to attack the sexual organs in a way that no one had ever seen before. She was over heated, and feened to be sexed.

Stevo pulled his fingers out of her. "N'all, fuck that. We ain't finna do that shit. You're my people. Sasha, get yo ass in here and handle her for me. Now!"

"No!" Jada snapped. "I'm fine. Just let me lay here for a minute. I'll be alright." She closed her thighs around her hand. "I'm okay, Stevo. Just sit here with me for a minute."

Stevo watched Jada rub all over her pussy until she passed out with her legs wide. As soon as she was out, he called Sasha into the room and fucked her from the back while he kept his eyes trained on Jada's pussy lips. He could see slight traces of her pinkness, and it drove him crazy, as much as he hated to admit it.

Chapter 9

Later that night, Makaroni grabbed four of his young shooters and rolled out to Washington Park. He pulled up in a Benz Wagon with two shooters in his backseat, and a Ford Expedition with two shooters in it with assault rifles on their laps. It was dark all over the park with the exception of the parking lot.

Stevo stood outside of his Bentley truck and waited for Makaroni to pull into the lot. He had ten men standing behind him that were dressed in all black with black ski masks on their faces. Each man was armed with two hand pistols, and Stevo had three Dracos inside of his truck already fully loaded, and ready to go.

Makaroni jumped out of his truck and stepped into the middle of the parking lot. He held his arms out. "Dis how we getting down now? You need a whole mafuckin' army just to meet up with me now, nigga?"

Stevo stepped away from his Hittas and smiled. He looked back at them. "Dis ain't my fault. They honor me as a king. Every last one of these vicious animals are eating off of my plate. Are you not supposed to expect for them to protect the ma'fucka that's feeding them?"

Makaroni eyed him and nodded. "Nigga, I guess." He walked closer to Stevo. "So, what? We finna broadcast our business in front of all of these niggas? Or we finna walk and talk and get an understanding?"

"It's however you wanna do shit, Homeboy. You wanna talk, we can talk. You wanna shoot? Shid, we can do that shit, too."

Makaroni scoffed. "Let's talk and see where shit go. Come on."

Stevo looked back at his crew of savages. "Yo, I'm finna walk, my niggas. Get them scopes out. Anythang look fishy, finger fuck them bitches like prom dates. You feel me?"

Makaroni wanted to step up and bust him in this shit. But instead of exposing his anger, he laughed it off. "We been homies since we were kids, and that's the order you give yo niggas? Really?"

"Ain't nothing personal. Just business. Let's roll."

They walked toward the middle of the big park and wound up by the picnic tables. Makaroni cleared his throat and turned to face Stevo. "Awright, I'm just finna cut to the chase. Montana said that you put hands on her, and that if Kandace wouldn't have popped yo ass, then you would have killed her. How true is that?"

Stevo snickered. "I did put hands on her, but not to fuck her up or nothing. I was disciplining one of my hoez and she got in my business. She was running her mouth like you know Montana do, and all I did was slam her ass to the ground after she rushed at me. I didn't punch her, slap her or none of that shit. Far as killing her; man, that's like my sister. I would never even think about doing some shit like that." He lied. Montana was right. Stevo was dead set on killing her had Kandace not have blindsided him. "So, this is why you agreed to meet me? To ask me this shit?"

Makaroni didn't know how to really feel about Stevo's answers. The fact that he had admitted to putting his hands on Montana was enough to vex Makaroni. He imagined him slamming his sister to the ground and thought about blowing his head off. He took Montana's mouth into consideration. She had always disliked Stevo, so he could see how she might have gotten out of pocket with him. Especially if he was whooping on a female. "N'all, bruh, the reason I agreed to come is because we niggas. We need to get an understanding real quick so we can get back to this money. I ain't heard from JaMichael in a few days. I don't know what he got going on down south, but we can't allow for that shit to affect us up here. The plug on the Rebirth still coming through strongly, but I don't know how much longer it will be that way. We gotta either assist his ass down there, or find a way to branch off from the Rebirth and do our own thing."

"I ain't giving up the Rebirth, Makaroni. That shit got the city going crazy. I got so many customers that I feel like I can never go broke. But now that I got them, and I've seen the amount of money I can make, it's like I want more. More money. More customers. More killas working behind me. More everything. Nigga, I been broke my whole life. I ain't going back there. If worse come to worse, I'll take my army down there and we'll tear Memphis up with no mercy. Kill JaMichael. Phoenix. And even Jahliya if we have to. Fuck it. Now, how do that sound?"

Makaroni mugged him. "Them are my people. I ain't finna let nothing like that happen to them." He looked over his shoulder and saw Stevo's people eyeing them closely. His entire crew was facing them. He turned back to Stevo. "So, what's good wit' us, bruh? Are we beefing or some shit? Nigga, is it still love?"

Stevo rubbed his chin. "That depends. You gon' hand over that lil' bitch that hit me up?"

"I ain't got her. That shit ain't have nothin' to do wit' me. Fuck you think I'll be holding her for?"

Stevo stepped into his face. "Nigga, you ain't gotta have her. Montana do. The streets talk. They say Montana and that bitch supposed to be forming some kind of female Cartel. And that you funding and supplying them hoez with the Rebirth, too. That true?"

"Nigga, that ain't yo business. You asked me if I was holding her, and I ain't. Far as what I'm doing wit' my money and my side of the Rebirth, that's my business. My question to you was, are we still good, or are we beefing? Simple as that."

Stevo felt offended. "Nigga, do you know who I am now? You talking to me like I'm one of them worker ass niggas in the parking lot back there. You better approach me with some ma'fuckin' respect. Fuck you thought this was?"

Makaroni stepped into his grill. "Nigga, you my ma'fuckin' brother. I love you to death, Stevo, but if you don't simmer yo ass down we can most definitely take it there. You letting this money and that lil' power you got go to yo head. You need to come back down to earth. Pride always comes before the fall. Never forget that."

"N'all, nigga, you need to calm up and respect my gangsta. I'm a ma'fuckin' god. Niggas a kill at the drop of a hat for me." He pressed his forehead to Makaroni's. "When I catch Kandace, I'm smoking that bitch, and whoever wit' her. So, you betta think wisely about funding her, or who you allow to be around her. Bullets ain't got no names on 'em." He laughed but was dead serious.

Makaroni clenched his jaw. "If anything happen to my sister, or any ma'fucka that's working under me, there will be some lethal consequences. I can promise you that." Makaroni felt himself becoming heated.

Stevo looked into his eyes. "Nigga, I said what I said." He stepped back and walked away from Makaroni. "For the record, love don't live here anymore."

Makaroni watched him walk away to the parking lot. To the other onlookers, they saw Stevo as a grown man of twenty, but Makaroni saw him as a boy of eight years old. He saw his best friend and the only brother he had ever known. His heart broke in two. He didn't know what would become of them, but he wasn't about to play no games with Stevo or his crew.

Later that same night, he knocked on Montana's apartment door with a heavy heart. She opened it in a pair of white boy shorts and a tank top. He strolled inside and went right to her bedroom. He took his shirt off and stripped down to his boxers. He slid under the covers.

Minutes after locking up, Montana followed him into the room. She got under the covers with him and laid on her side facing him. She rubbed his soft cheek. "Makaroni, what's the matter? Something is wrong. I can feel it."

Makaroni had so many things going through his mind that he didn't know where to start. He felt his eyes burning. He closed them, fighting back the tears that threatened to sail down his cheeks. "Ever since I been old enough to know what a friend or a brother was, that's what Stevo has been to me. Now we ain't shit. I just lost my nigga today."

Montana immediately disconnected herself from conversation at the hearing of Stevo's name. She felt nothing but anger and irritation. "That's who has you feeling like shit right now?"

"It's deeper than that. You see, not only have I lost my brother and right-hand mans, but I think I'm gon' wind up being the one that take him out of the Game." Hearing himself admit those things to Montana caused a tear to drop from his eye. He loved his homey. Always had. They had been through hell and back together. He never thought he would see the day when they were on the other side of the fence from each other.

Montana saw the tear seep. She kissed it and wiped the rest away with her thumb. "It's hard for me to empathize with you about him, Makaroni, but I hate seeing you hurt.

When you hurt, I hurt. I'd do anything to take your pain away." She kissed his eyelids.

Makaroni kept them closed. He took a deep breath. "Yo, I know you ain't never heard a man say this before, but sis, I need to just hold you. We ain't gotta talk. We ain't gotta do nothing more than me holding you. For me, that would be everything. I need you. I feel so fuckin' weak right now."

Montana nodded in understanding. She turned her back to him and snuggled as close to him as she could. She pulled his arm around herself. "I love you, Mack. You are strong. I don't know what exactly you're feeling, but I know that the hurt will pass. You will be better soon. I'll be here to hold you down every step of the way. I promise."

Makaroni held her tighter. He knew that he needed to release Stevo. He could see in Stevo's eyes that he looked to do Montana bodily harm. He saw the snake in him. He couldn't allow for him to hurt his sister. He would rather die first. He kissed Montana's cheek. "I love you, Montana. I'll never let a nigga hurt you again. Never. I'm sorry for not being there when you needed me to be. I'm sorry for letting Stevo hurt you." His voice began to crack. He was trying all he could to convince himself that Stevo's intentions were to harm Montana. It was the only way he could release him from his heart.

"It's not your fault, Makaroni. I know that if you would have been there, he would've never laid a hand on me. I know that you will go above and beyond to make sure that I am well taken care of. That's why I love you so much. I truly, truly do." She rubbed the top of his wrist.

His arms tightened around her body. "We ain't gon' be in this hood forever, Montana. I swear we ain't. I ain't gon' always have to slang this bullshit in order to make things happen for our family. I'ma find another way. I'ma switch the Game up real soon. I got to."

Montana smiled in the darkness. She believed every word that came out of his mouth. She always felt that Makaroni's heart was pure along with his intentions to do the best he could using whatever he had. Makaroni wasn't an evil man like she felt Stevo was. When her brother did things it was because he had a set goal in mind. There was always a method to his madness, and she had watched Makaroni show remorse for many of the wrong things he had done. She felt that deep inside of him was a good person. A person that he wanted to be more than the evil one that he was forced to be at times. "You know, Makaroni? I believe you. I know your heart, and I know it's pure. You do whatever you need to do, and I promise to be right here standing beside you through it all. I love you so much."

Makaroni held her tighter. "Damn, I'm sick, sis. I gotta get some sleep. I love you, too, and I'll talk to you in the morning. Night, night."

"Night, night, Mack."

Ghost

Chapter 10

Two days later, Jada came staggering out of the bedroom with her hair all over the place. She felt weak. In less than four full days, she lost five pounds. She hadn't eaten in two full days. The Rebirth prevented her from having an appetite. All she craved was more of the potent drug. She came into the living room where Sasha was sitting watching music videos on the 4K television. She fell to her knees in front of her. "Sasha, where is my brother? I need him."

She sucked her teeth and looked down on Jada with envy and irritation. Ever since Jada came into the picture Stevo had given her all of the attention. He acted as if Sasha was nothing more than a slave and after thought. Sasha ignored Jada.

Jada's mouth felt like she'd bee chewing on sand. It was so dry. She smacked her lips and drew up spit to wet it a bit. Her cotton mouth made her words almost hurt. "Sasha?" She croaked. "Please, tell me where Stevo is. I need him."

"Bitch, the world don't revolve around you." Sasha snapped.

Jada sat on her folded legs. She ran her fingers through her hair. She looked around the room to see if she could spot Stevo's jacket anywhere. When she was unable to find it, she became sick. The stomach pains resonated all over her abdomen like cramps. She felt nauseous. "Did he leave anything for me?"

Sasha mugged her. "He might have. But like I said, the world don't revolve around you."

In actuality, Stevo had left two full syringes of the Rebirth with Sasha. He had given her strict orders. When Jada woke up, she was supposed to make her shower and eat something. Then she was to give Jada one of the syringes. Those were his commands.

"Well, if he gave you somethin' for me, can I have it? Please?" Jada asked in her sweetest tone. She was feeling woozy. She needed a fix. Her head was pounding as if somebody was stomping on it with boots.

Sasha stood up. "I don't know why Stevo so obsessed with you. Bitch, you ain't even all that. Look at you. You definitely ain't got shit on me. I bet yo hair ain't even real, is it?" Sasha laughed, and pulled her on her hair as hard as she could. "You see this shit, bitch? This shit growing out of my head. Ain't shit fake over here. That nappy shit you got going on is fake as a three-dollar bill."

Jada didn't care that Sasha was talking about her. Her hair was real, and it was longer than Sasha's. But she just didn't care. She came to the conclusion that Sasha was jealous of her. She needed to ease her jealousy so she could get what Stevo left her. "Sasha, you're beautiful. I can't hold a candle to you. I would never try to step on your toes. He's just my brother. That's it. I swear that's all."

"Yeah, right. Bitch, I see how he looks at you. He look at you like you're God's gift to the world. He ain't touched me nor has he been the same with me ever since you came around. It's your fault. Why won't you just leave us alone?"

Jada felt a contraction go through her. It hurt so bad that she doubled over in pain. "Please, Sasha. You gotta know what I'm going through here. Please, give me that fucking drug!"

"Bitch, what you gon' do for me, huh? Everything ain't always gotta be about you. What are you going to do for Sasha! Huh, bitch?"

Jada placed her forehead to the floor. "Anything. Any. Thing. Just please, give it to me."

Sasha smiled. She kicked off her sandal. She hadn't showered in a few days. She knew her feet were sweaty, and maybe even a bit funky. "Kiss my feet, bitch. Come on."

Jada looked up at her. "Are you serious?"

"As serious as you wanting this dope." She held out her right foot and wiggled her toes. "Here you go."

Sasha crawled across the floor. She stopped in front of Jada and knelt down. She caught a slight whiff of her feet and was taken aback. She looked up at her.

"Fuck is you waiting on?"

Jada closed her eyes, and kissed Sasha's feet. First the right one, and then the left. When she finished she looked up at her. "Now, can I please have it?"

Sasha sat on the couch and crossed her thighs. "Jada, you always begging Stevo to let you go. Why the fuck won't you just leave now that he isn't here? Wouldn't that make all of the sense in the world?"

Jada willed herself to stand up. "Sasha, I ain't answering no more of your questions. He didn't leave you with anything for me. You're just taking advantage of me right now. It's so unbecoming of you."

"Un-be what of me?" Sasha asked. "Bitch, whatever." She grabbed her purse. "If he ain't leave nothin' for you then what is this?" She pulled out two syringes wrapped in a Zip-loc bag and taped up.

Jada felt her stomach growl. She grew dizzy yet was excited at the same time. Now that she knew it was there she wanted it. She was willing to go through Sasha to get it. She stepped closer to her and held out her hand. "Stevo left that for me. Give it to me."

Sasha stood up with her purse. "I ain't giving you shit. Jump yo ass down and kiss my feet again. Now!"

Jada shook her head. She balled up her fists. "Okay then. If this is how you want to play things. She rushed her at full speed and tackled her over the couch. They fell with a loud thud. Jada landed on top of Sasha. She pulled at the purse.

Sasha twisted her hips, and bucked Jada off of her. She threw the purse into the hallway and rushed Jada with swinging fists. "Bitch, why don't you just run away and never come back?" She tried to knock her head off.

Jada slid between her thighs and jumped up. She ran as fast as she could and grabbed the purse. She was halfway to her bedroom when Sasha tackled her by the waist. She fell to the floor groaning. Sasha rained down punches on the back of her head. Blow after blow. "Leave. I hate you. I don't want you here."

Jada twisted around and punched Sasha as hard as she could, busting her nose. Sasha flew backward. She jumped up with blood dripping from her lips. She screamed and ran at Jada again. Jada grabbed the purse and hurried inside of her room. She locked the door and sat with her back to it. She licked her inner forearm and pulled one of the syringes from the purse. She found her thickest veins and injected the Rebirth into it while Sasha kicked on the door and sent one threat after the next. A smile spread across Jada's face, and then she was nodding.

***

Makaroni sat in the middle of the living room of one of his Trap houses overseeing the operation. He had four square tables inside of the living room. At each table was four workers. They chopped up the Rebirth and placed different quantities into small Ziploc bags. When the small Ziploc bags were filled. They were weighed and placed inside of another bag for distribution. Every hour his distributors would come and pick up the work and flood the streets with it. Even though Makaroni had yet to hear back from JaMichael or Jahliya, Rubio's people kept the Rebirth coming at a steady rate. Makaroni made sure that Rubio got every penny he was owed on time. He didn't know how Stevo was carrying on with his side of the operations, but he imagined just as well since they had not been given any warnings by Rubio's Cartel. Makaroni checked the time on his phone it read 11:15pm. He told Montana that he would meet her at her place at midnight. If he wanted to keep that promise, then he needed to get a move on.

"Yo, everything look good. Y'all keep this shit up. Shut it down at three." He nodded to his security that kept an eye on his business. "Got that?" They nodded and went back to eyeing the workers to make sure that everything was on the straight and narrow.

As Makaroni was about to get into his G Wagon, he heard fast footsteps approaching, and somebody calling his name. "Makaroni! Makaroni! Please, don't go!" Came the voice. His security upped their weapons. The street was quiet and desolate. Dark with the exception of one streetlamp in the middle of the block a ways down. Makaroni squinted in time to see a twelve-year-old boy running up to him. He stopped halfway. "Please, Makaroni. I don't have any more money. I wish I did, but I don't." He hollered.

Makaroni was confused. "Money for what, lil' homie?"

"The Rebirth. I need it. I'm so sick, and so is my sister. She been throwing up a lot." He reported.

Makaroni's stomach dropped. He walked toward the little boy concerned. "Lil' man, you doing this shit?"

The boy nodded. "My whole house is. It's all we got. My mama don't buy food no more. All she buy is your work, but we ran out. I can't take the pain. Neither can my sister. Please help us, Mr. Makaroni." He begged. He fell to his knees.

Makaroni rushed to his side and helped him up. He was devastated. He started to wonder in that moment was it all worth it? The money. The power. The lifestyle. Was it all worth it if he was going to be destroying the lives of innocent children? He questioned everything. "Lil' homie, jump in my whip. We about to go to yo' crib so I can see what the hell is going on."

When they pulled up in front of the little boy's house ten minutes later, Makaroni was shocked to see that the boy's home was right next door to an abandoned building that had at one time been a community center before the city closed it down due to budget cuts. Now, Makaroni's trap stars posted up in front of it and served his Rebirth all around the clock. The boy got out of the truck and rushed up the steps. He beat on the door. Seconds later, his eleven-year-old sister answered it with her hair all over her head. She had bags under her eyes and appeared severely underweight. Her lips were white.

"Makaroni, this is my sister Shell. She's a year younger than me." The boy said.

Shell waved. "Hi."

Makaroni knelt in front of her. "How are you doing, lil' lady?"

"I'm sick. I need some of that stuff my brother be sniffing. Mama ain't here." She pushed open the door and walked into the house.

Makaroni nodded at his security to be on point. He stepped into the house and crushed an empty beer can under his feet. It smelled like piss and feces. A skinny cat ran past his foot and into the night. He ventured further into the house and looked around disgusted. It not only smelled deplorable, but it was filthy. There was one big couch with holes all over it. The pillows were on the floor with roaches crawling all

94

over them. A series of mice scampered over the trash that was on the floor. It was freezing inside.

Shell sat on a pillow filled with roaches. "I'll suck your thing if you want me to, Makaroni. I know how. My mama showed me how to make money for her."

Makaroni frowned and wanted to kill her parents. He looked down to her brother. "Lil' homie, what's your name?"

"My name Yummy. Why?"

"Look, Yummy, what time you think yo' mother comin' be back?"

"She ain't been here in two days. She might not come back for a while. Are you gon' hook us up with the Rebirth?" Yummy asked.

Makaroni didn't know what to do. He knew that both children were dope-sick. He didn't want to leave them that way, yet he didn't want them on his drugs either. He felt lower than dirt. "Look, Yummy, I'ma get y'all right tonight, but after that I wanna work on weening y'all off of this dope, man. How does that sound?"

Yummy didn't care what he intended on doing tomorrow. As long has he took care of him and Shell in the moment. The Rebirth was calling him like never before. "That sound cool, man. Just please take care of us."

Shell walked over to him. "Do you want me to do anything for you?" She started to reach for his crotch.

Makaroni caught her hand and knelt, killing two roaches that were too slow in their retreat. "Listen to me, lil' sistah, you are a Princess. You ain't supposed to be doing none of what your mother has you doing. You're too young to be doing drugs, and even thinking about sex. So no, I don't need you to do anything for me. When was the last time you ate anything?"

She shrugged. "I don't know."

Yummy stepped forward. "It's been a few days. Things are crazy around here."

The cat came back into the house and took off running behind the three mice. The rodents scurried into different directions. The cat stopped in the kitchen doorway and hissed. Its ears turned backward. It slowly stepped backward. Two big, black, red-eyed rats slowly came out of the kitchen and hissed at the cat. The cat looked back at them and took off running outside the open front door.

Makaroni shook his head in disgust. "Look, I'm finna put y'all up for a few days. When your mother come back, I'ma have one of my workers holler at her. We gon' see if we can get her any help. This ain't living right here. Especially not for you and your little sister."

Shell walked up to Makaroni and took his hand. "You're a good person, Makaroni. I like you a lot." She smiled. Her face was dirty.

Makaroni pulled her to him and wrapped his arm around her upper back. "It's all good, Shell. We gon' figure things out. Let's go."

Chapter 11

After two weeks with no updates of what was taking place between JaMichael and Phoenix down south, Stevo got a call from Rubio Flores letting him know that he would be in Chicago, Illinois for two days, and that he wanted to meet up with him and Makaroni as soon as he touched down. Stevo sent Makaroni a text letting him know what the deal was, but it wasn't needed because Rubio had also gotten into contact with Makaroni and gave him the same message he'd given Stevo.

On the afternoon that Stevo was set to drive down to Chicago, Jada ran out of the solution for her inhaler. Instead of allowing for her to go out and fill her own prescription, Stevo figured he would take care of it himself. He loaded Sasha into the truck and started off for the Walgreen's pharmacy. His phone was buzzing like crazy with order after order for the Rebirth. As soon as he got through with the customer, he rerouted the call to a distributor of his that was closest to the client. This went on the entire way to Walgreen's.

It was a bright and sunny afternoon. He parked his truck inside of Walgreen's parking lot and placed his Chanel sunglasses over his eyes to block out the harmful rays of the sun. "Shorty, gone in there and fill this prescription for her inhaler. As soon as it's filled, bring yo ass right back out here so we can go. I gotta get down to Chicago as soon as possible. Don't hold me up."

Sasha nodded. "Okay, daddy." She took the prescription from him and started to open the door to the truck. Her eyes got low. She brought her hand over them to block the sun that was shining directly in through the windshield. "Daddy, ain't that Kandace right there?" She pointed across the street directly from Walgreen's.

Stevo nearly snapped his neck to see where she was pointing. He followed her index finger. Sure enough, Kandace sat on the hood of a black Benz with her cell phone glued to her ear. She nodded her head and kept talking. Stevo wondered who she was talking to. He looked her up and down. She looked fresh. She was fitted from head to toe in a Yves St. Laurent pink and white outfit, with a pair of matching Balenciaga's. The designer gear only added to his irritation. Somebody was making sure that she was up to par. He hated seeing that. The first person he thought about was Montana. He clenched his jaw over and over trying to decide what he was about to do.

"That is her though, right?" Sasha asked looking at him.

He nodded and scanned the busy street. They were in a small shopping district. There were shoppers walking in and out of the stores all around them. There was no way for him to blast Kandace without being seen. He had to be smart, as much as he hated to be. "Yeah, that's that bitch."

Sasha nodded as she watched the sun shimmer off of Kandace's lip gloss. "I thought that was her. She look good. I wonder why the Rebirth ain't fuckin' her up like it's doing everybody else?" Sasha thought out loud.

Stevo was in a murderous zone. With every breath Kandace took it caused his blood to boil. He wanted her life. He wanted to take her out of the Game. He felt betrayed and belittled by what she and Montana did to him. There was no doubt in his mind that he had been set up. He texted the license plates to the Benz into his phone. "Shorty, run in there and get my sister inhaler. Hurry up though. If you come out here and I'm gone that's because I took off after this bitch, but I'll be back. Just be cool. You hear me?"

Sasha frowned. She didn't want to be stranded. "Daddy, why don't I just stay with you until you handle her ass? We can always get Jada asthma medicine later."

"Because, bitch, you not running shit. I am. Now, I done told you what to do. Go do it." He ordered.

Sasha climbed out of the truck and slammed the door. She mugged Stevo. For a second she felt like cursing him out. She was tired of his rough handling of her. She wondered how it was that he expected for her to be so loyal to him if he always wanted to handle her as if hated her. It was starting to get old. She was feeling more and more disconnected from him emotionally.

Stevo waited until Sasha walked into Walgreen's before he turned his attention back to Kandace. She pulled open the passenger's door and stepped inside of the car. Seconds later he saw her older brother Dexter appear. Dexter had long dread locks that fell to his waist. He was dark skinned with brown eyes. Six feet even, and two hundred solid pounds. His neck was flooded with gold chains. Stevo nodded. "Aiight then. I got both of they ass." He pulled the Tech from under his driver's seat and drove out of the parking lot at the same time Dexter pulled away from the clothing store he'd been shopping inside.

***

"Mama? Mama? Where you at?" Makaroni called stepping into Maisey's home. He tossed his keys on the table in the front room and went in search of his mother. He could smell the stench of marijuana. He found that odd. He knew that Maisey didn't allow for anybody to smoke in her home. But it didn't take him long for him to find out just who was smoking the Ganja. He found Maisey sitting at the dining room table with a fat joint in her hand. She brought the joint to her mouth and pulled from it. The cherry turned a bright red. Then she took it from her mouth and inhaled the smoke.

Makaroni stepped in front of her. "My Queen, what's the matter?" He kissed her soft cheek.

Maisey exhaled the smoke. On the table before her was a platter full of rolled joints of Sativa Cannabis. Her eyes were low. She was now high enough to speak freely with her son. "Baby, have a seat. We need to talk."

Makaroni was worried. He was praying that she wasn't about to give him any devastating news in regards to her health. He couldn't imagine what that bit of news would do to him. "What's up, mama?"

She blew smoke to the ceiling and stubbed out the joint in the ashtray. "I think I'm finally ready to tell you what really happened between me and your father, Makaroni." She exhaled and looked up into his penetrating eyes.

Makaroni let out a sigh of relief. "Man. You had me worried like crazy, ma. I didn't know what was going on." He reached across the table and took a hold of her hand. "It's good. You can talk to me."

She lowered her head and tried to gather up the courage to say what she was about to say. "Baby, I need you to know that I love you, and I love Montana with all of my heart. Y'all should know that I would never do anything to intentionally hurt you. Your mother is not perfect. I have made a lot of mistakes, but I had changed for the better. Understand that." She blew air out and shook her head.

"It's okay, mama. Just tell me." Makaroni rubbed the back of her hand.

She looked up at him. "Okay, baby. Let's just go for the gusto. Firstly, Howard is not your biological father. He's not yours, nor is he Montana's."

Makaroni released her hand and sat back. "What? Then who is our father?"

Maisey took a second to get her wordings right. She was sure that she would go to the grave with all of their family secrets. Now for some reason she felt compelled to tell Makaroni everything. "I met your father while he was doing a short bid in the Tennessee State Penitentiary. I used to work in that place as a nurse. I'll spare the details. Long story short, prior to him coming there, he and I had went to high school together in Memphis. We had a small thing as kids, and when I met him in their things sort of took off again. We couldn't do much, but the times when we were able to do what we did, we wound up making you." She took a second before she moved forward. She grabbed the joint and relit it. Smoke billowed to the ceiling.

Makaroni didn't know what to do. He was lost. He needed to know more. "Okay, so then what? What is his name? Is he still alive? Does he know about me?"

Maisey shook her head. "No, he doesn't know about you. And yes, he's still alive."

"Okay den, so what's his name?" Makaroni needed to know. He wanted to see if he was on Facebook. He wanted to see what he looked like. Now that Howard was no longer his father it made him feel hopeful.

"Your father's name is Phoenix."

Makaroni stood up. "Phoenix Stevens-Mitchell? The same nigga that tried to kill us over in Orange Mound?"

Maisey stood up. "Baby, I wanted to tell you as soon as Jahliya told me about who you guys were going to war with down there. That's the reason neither her nor JaMichael has called you back down there. I don't want you warring against your father. All of this violence needs to cease. You two need to sit down and get an understanding of who each other is.

As it stands, the only person outside of me that knows he's your father is Jahliya, and she just found out two days ago. I told her to keep it from JaMichael."

Makaroni was lost. He paced back and forth in front of his mother. "How could he be my father though? He don't even look like he that old."

Maisey smiled. "Your father has always been a looker. He looks thirty, but Phoenix is forty-three years old. He just carries it well." She stopped smiling when she saw the angry expression on her son's face. "I'm sorry, baby."

"And Montana. Is that her father, too?" He stepped closer to his mother.

"Well, you two are only minutes apart, so you tell me." She didn't understand that question.

"Mama, come on. You know what I mean."

"Yes, baby, he is her father as well." She grabbed his hands. "Are you mad at me?"

Makaroni didn't know how to feel. On the one hand, Howard had barely ever been there for them anyway. He hadn't loved the man in a long time. So, he felt blank when it came to no longer having any attachments to him. On the other hand, Phoenix had never been given the opportunity to get to know him, so he couldn't blame their nonexistent relationship on anybody other than his mother, yet he loved her way too much to hold anything against her. So, he simply had to let his anger go no matter how small it was. "I hope you gon' be the one to break all this down to Montana."

"I will. I plan on telling her tonight."

"Wait, so how did Howard come into play in the first place?" Makaroni wanted to make sure that he had the full story so he could put it all behind him.

"We were married when I fell in love with Phoenix. Around that time, we were going through a really rough patch. Your father fell in love with a coworker while we were still together, and I fell in love with Phoenix. We both had children on each other during our marriage. We were kids, and very immature. Our marriage was forced by our families who were devout Jehovah's Witnesses. They found out that Howard and I were screwing and made us wed. It was a crazy time, but that's what it is."

Makaroni nodded. "Well, at least now I know." He hugged her. "You're still perfect to me. I would never allow for anything that you did in the past alter my love for you. You are my rock." He kissed her forehead.

Maisey smiled. She stepped back. "The screwing between you and Montana comes from that side of your DNA. All of your father's family get down like that. Their business is all over Memphis. Everybody know about the Stevens'." She lowered her head. "My side of the family ain't so perfect either though but that's another story. The bottom line is that you too have to fight those urges for each other. Y'all used to be kissing and hugging when you were just three years old. The daycare lady used to tell me that all the time. You have always been overprotective of Montana. She was just as crazy about you, too. But if y'all think y'all gon' be fuckin' and all of that while I got the knowledge that you're doing it, you got another thang coming. I'll kill the both of you. I mean that. Now, you ain't in love with that girl, is you?"

"Yeah, I love my sister. Why would you even ask me that?" He felt himself becoming irritated.

"No, honey, I'm not asking you if you love her. I asked if you were *in* love with her. Those are two different things."

Montana stepped into the living room with her fists balled up at her sides. She'd been listening to their conversation for the last twenty minutes. She stepped out of the darkness. "Why does it even matter to you what we do, mama?"

Huh?" She was furious. She hated that Maisey felt the need to poke her nose into their relationship. They weren't kids anymore, and their bodies belonged to them. She felt that Maisey needed to stay in her own lane.

"Montana, I can understand if you are feeling some type of way because of what I said, but you are still going to approach me with the utmost respect. That is my right as your mother."

"Why should I though, mama? We are twenty years old and you are just telling us who our father is. How wrong is that?" Montana fired back.

"You're right, baby. I was wrong for that, and I am sorry. But that still doesn't give you the right to disrespect me." Maisey felt a bit tongue tied. She really didn't know what she could have possibly said to an upset Montana. She wanted to get her own point across, but she felt so guilty for what had transpired between her and Phoenix that she didn't know what to say.

"I would never disrespect you. I love you way too much. I just don't want you dictating my life, and his either. We love each other how we want. It works for us. That's all that should matter."

Makaroni stepped to Montana and turned his back to Maisey. "Shorty, chill, we good. You and I will get an understanding later. Right now, we need to process this whole Phoenix thing."

"An understanding about what? Y'all need to be brother and sister, that is it. Anything outside of that is unnatural. It's not happening, so get that shit out of ya'll minds."

Montana smacked her lips. "I need some fresh air. While I'm gone, please don't try and turn Makaroni against me. Thank you." Makaroni tried to hold her, but she jerked away from him. She grabbed her jacket and slammed the front door.

Maisey wanted to kick her tail. "Boy, you betta go get her before I kill her."

Makaroni laughed. "Y'all so much alike it's crazy." He hugged Maisey.

"More than you know." She hugged him back. "I love you baby, and again, I'm sorry. I wish I would have told you sooner. But now, it's out in the open. Go get that girl and comfort her before she do somethin' stupid. No more sex though. Okay?"

Makaroni nodded. "Yes, ma'am."

Chapter 12

"But seeing as you already got a plug on the dog food, I'ma put you in with this girly-girl so you and your lil' homies can make somethin' shake with that. Montana say that Rebirth that Makaroni hitting y'all with should have you seeing five thousand every week. This girl will push you up to about eight thousand when it's all said and done. We ain't rocking shit up either. We gone leave it as powder, and let ma'fuckas step on it however they want. Once you get to rocking shit up, that's when you find yourself in a trap, and confined to the ghetto. I want you to have your mind outside of the ghetto at all times. You gotta think big." Dexter took a sip of his drink through his straw as he sat across from Kandace. They were seated at an outside diner by the name of Big Boy's. He picked up his double cheeseburger and took a bite out of it.

Kandace picked at her French fries. She felt a slight migraine approaching. She didn't know if it was from the bright sunlight, or if it was from the effects of her trying to kick the Rebirth. She'd just popped two Percocet pills to get the feeling of numbness that the Rebirth always gave her. She was treating the Percocet as a form of a nicotine patch. Every second of every day the Rebirth called out to her and promised her all of the delights of her heart. She ignored it. She needed her strength. It was the most important thing in the world to her outside of her moneybag.

"Girl, are you listening to what I'm saying?" Dexter asked. He dunked the fries into his ketchup and ate them.

"Yeah, bro, I hear you. My mind was just reeling for a minute." She slid her black Sunglasses over her eyes and picked up her cheeseburger.

"What you thinking about? Keaira?" Dexter felt his throat go tight. The authorities had yet to find out what had taken place with Keaira. They didn't know if she was dead, missing, or had run away. Though there was an open investigation into her disappearance, the trail had already run cold.

"N'all, I be trying to forget about her because it hurt too bad to sit around and think about her all day long. I just hope that wherever she is, she is okay." Kandace lied. She knew that her sister was dead and gone. Every time she thought about her, she felt guilty. She hated herself for how things had transpired.

"I'm sure they'll find her soon. I still think that nigga Stevo got somethin' to do with her disappearance. Keaira used to tell me all the time while I was in the County Jail how her and that nigga stayed into it, and how he wasn't helping out with Steven. It's so many trifling niggas in this world that it's ridiculous. The only reason I got hope that Keaira is still alive is because I know how much she loved Steven. She would never go anywhere without him. So, I know that they are together."

The more Dexter talked, the sicker she felt. She already knew that Keaira was deceased. Now she wondered if her nephew Steven was also. She had never gotten the full scoop on what had taken place with Steven. Knowing that Stevo was involved, she expected the worse. "Dexter, let's change the subject. This topic is getting me depressed as hell." She wrapped up her Burger and threw it in the trash. The sun began to set quickly. As it faded away, it brought on the night's chill.

Dexter zipped up his jacket. "Yeah, maybe you're right. Let's get up out of here." He downed his juice and tossed all of his garbage into the trash.

Kandace made it to the car first. She pulled open the door, and sighed, closing her eyes. She felt so low. Keaira's face played over her closed eyelids. "Damn, Keaira, I miss you so much." She took her pistol from the small of her back and placed it on her lap.

Dexter stopped outside of the car to smoke a Newport. Smoking a cigarette was best for him right after he ate a meal. Kandace knocked on the glass and threw her arms up. He held up one finger. "Hold on, sis." He showed her the cigarette." She waved him off and sat back in her seat. She placed her ear buds into her ears and turned on Ella Mai's *Down*.

Stevo parked his truck on the side of the restaurant closer to the alley. He got out with a ski mask over his face, and black gloves on his hands. He dropped to the ground with the Tech .9 and scampered across the concrete staying low as possible. He could already taste the kills. His heart started to pound in his chest. He cocked the Tech and made haste in the direction of Dexter and Kandace.

Dexter took a long pull from his cigarette. He flicked it away and inhaled the smoke for a few seconds. He blew it out and dropped a drip of cologne into his hands. He hated the way cigarettes made his fingers and clothes smelled. He rubbed the cologne all over him and allowed for the breeze to whisk it away. When he felt that he was good he pulled open the car door.

"Dang, nigga, it took you long enough." Kandace snapped. She grabbed his hat off of the driver's seat so he could sit down. Before she could throw it into the back of the car, she heard Stevo's running feet on the sidewalk. She looked up as saw the ski mask approaching. She cocked her gun. "Dexter!"

Dexter looked down at her. "Girl, what are you screaming about?" He felt Stevo slam the Tech into the back of his head hard, busting it.

Then Stevo pulled the trigger like a vicious assassin. *Bock! Bock! Bock! Bock!* Dexter's head rattled around on his neck over and over as the slugs shot through his skull and big chunks of his brain were knocked out of him. He twisted around to face a masked Stevo. Stevo fired more shots and slung him to the ground. He popped him twice more just to overkill him. He had never truly liked Dexter. Dexter had many opportunities to put both he and Makaroni on, but he never did. Because he didn't, Stevo hated him enough to overkill him. Stevo stepped over his dead body and looked into the car to find it empty. He rose, and saw Kandace booking it across the busy street with a gun in her hand. She stopped halfway and turned around. *Boom! Boom! Boom! Boom!* Stevo ducked and crawled through the car. He blasted through the window, shattering the glass. *Bock! Bock! Bock! Bock!* He threw open the door and tried to make it across the busy street with cars blaring their horns, and angry truckers swerving out of the way to prevent hitting him.

Kandace continued to run as fast as she could. She looked over her shoulder to see Stevo stuck, trying to cross the busy road. She figured he would be stuck for a minute. She kept running. The image of her brother's murder played over and over in her brain. She felt sick, and so angry that she couldn't think straight.

***

Makaroni sat across from a smiling Stevo four hours later. Makaroni had two of his trusted shooters standing behind him at the ready. Stevo had two of his own. His shooters were both sixteen years old and were from the Village

Projects inside of Chicago, Illinois. Both youngsters had a few bodies a piece under their belt. Stevo rubbed his hands together. He rocked an iced-out Patek watch on his left wrist, and a gold bracelet dripped in diamonds on his right. He had three chains around his neck. All were splashing with diamonds. His Chanel sunglasses were gold-rimmed and shining. He rocked Chanel from head to toe.

Makaroni kept it simple. He had on all black Tom Ford pants and a matching black hoody sweater. Black Air Force ones, and he used his phone for a clock. After seeing the conditions of Yummy and Shell's place, he wanted to do better. He didn't feel right about splurging on himself when there were women and children dying off of the drugs that he was slanging. He wanted to do something different with his money. He just couldn't quite figure out what as of yet. He waited for Rubio to enter, avoiding Stevo's eye contact.

They were on the twentieth floor of the Waldorf Astoria in Chicago, Illinois. Their boardroom had a view of downtown Chicago. It was extremely bright and looked amazing to Makaroni. The view was enough to fool anybody that didn't know what the heart of Chicago was really all about. It was a dirty city full of back-alley politics, drug wars, and cold-blooded hustlers. He took a deep breath and shook his head. His brain had a hard time slowing down.

"Nigga, it's good. You can look over here at the god. See all this mafuckin' greatness. Dis what that money do for a nigga." He set his right hand on the table so the diamonds on his bracelet could dance. "Rich nigga shit."

Makaroni mugged him. "Nigga, how much of that money is you giving back to the community?"

Stevo was almost offended. "Not a muthafuckin' penny. The community ain't give me shit when I was down and out.

Why the fuck should I give the community any fuckin' thang?" He spat.

"Nigga, do you know that it's lil' kids out there dying off of our drugs? Huh?"

He nodded. "That's 'cause it's that sauce, nigga. If a m'a-fucka can't handle it then they shouldn't be indulging. You feel me?" He dusted off his sleeves.

"I'm tired of hurting everybody just so we can get ahead, Stevo. We are killing our people. I don't like what we are doing to the community." Makaroni didn't know why he was relaying all of these things to Stevo, but they were weighing so heavy on his heart. He wanted to do so much better. There had to be a way to take the money that they already had and turn it into something positive. His spirit was nagging at him to do the right thing. He had never felt his own soul condemning him so bad.

"Look nigga, miss me with that bullshit. My paper just starting to get right. I keep a comma like a run-on sentence now. Don't fuck that up. You got me?"

Makaroni nodded. "Yeah, nigga, I got you."

Rubio Flores stepped into the board room and took a seat at the head of the table. He sat a laptop in front of him. "Makaroni, Stevo, I like what the both of you have done so far. Our production in Wisconsin is up by ten percent since the two of you have been put in place there. I like hearing that. Unfortunately, we still have a major problem."

Stevo stood up. "Fuck you mean we got a problem?" He was high off of the Rebirth. There was no common sense inside his brain.

Rubio eyed him. "Stevo, why don't you have a seat? Don't interrupt me again. It's rude."

Stevo remained standing for a second, and then took a seat. His eyelids felt heavy. He tried his best to not nod out.

One of Rubio Flores's cardinal rules was that they weren't supposed to use the Rebirth. It was a rule that Stevo had broken right away.

"As I was saying, we still have a major problem that needs to be tended to right away. Unfortunately, both of your lives are at stake because it starts with your sources. Neither JaMichael nor Phoenix have been able to come to a conclusion, so now that leaves me with no choice. They both have to go if they have not reached an agreement by the end of this week. They must be annihilated, and I will officially become the sole controller of the Rebirth. When I take over to control, things will be running way differently to say the least."

"Like how?" Stevo asked curiously.

Rubio nodded to a short, beefy security guard of his Cartel. The muscle-bound Mexican man snatched Stevo up with blazing speed. He slammed him on top of the table. His face was a mask of fury. He placed his forearm under Stevo's chin choking him. Stevo's men didn't know what to do. They knew they were out of bounds, and one false move could cost them their lives. Stevo struggled against the cock-strong Latino.

Rubio Flores causally took out a cigar and lit the tip of it. He puffed on it and blew smoke to the ceiling. Behind his chair was a beautiful shot of the downtown Chicago skyline. "You are the first person that I have ever given so may warnings to, Stevo. It seems to me that you don't think that fat meat is greasy. When I tell you not interrupt me, that means that I do not wish to be interrupted. Do I make myself clear this time?"

The muscle-bound man released Stevo just a bit so he could respond. "Yeah, man. I got you. Call this steroid freak up off me."

Rubio nodded to his bodyguard. "Take your seat, Stevo."

Stevo was released. He straightened his clothes, and then his chains. He felt like he had been punked out. His pride was wounded it. He could no longer look across the table at Makaroni. He wanted to kill Rubio Flores for having hands laid upon him.

"Like I was saying; if there is no deal made between the two by Sunday, both JaMichael, and Phoenix will lose their lives. They will be replaced by a crew of my choosing. The Rebirth will be solely owned by me, and I will distribute it as I see fit. Now, the reason I brought you two here is because I have a proposition for the both of you. It is based off of your consistent numbers you've brought in since you have taken a stake of the Rebirth. If either one, or the both of you, can convince the pair of JaMichael and Phoenix to come to a understanding, I will leave the Rebirth within the hands of whichever man you two choose to lead it. Also, I will help the pair of you to venture out into Illinois, Minnesota, Iowa, Indiana, Missouri, and Michigan. You will be able to do to those states what you have been able to do within your own. You will have the Holy Grail of the Rebirth." He puffed on his cigar for a second. Then, he leaned forward. "Now, suppose no understanding can be reached between the two before Sunday. You two will have until this Saturday to take them both out of the Game. You annihilate them before I get the chance to, and I will structure a deal for the two of you. It will span six months at a time for the two of you to be in control of the Rebirth. Makaroni, this drug does originate from your family's bloodline, am I correct?"

"Yeah, it do." *More than you know.* He thought.

"That's all I have to say. Is there any questions?" He looked directly at Stevo.

"Why should we go through all of this bullshit of getting them pussy niggas to squash anything? Why can't we just smoke they ass, and keep it moving? You put us in control of the Rebirth, and we do what we been doing, but with more cities and troops. That's what makes sense to me."

"Because that shit would be bogus nigga, damn. Clearly, he made a deal with them to begin with. The man is trying to keep his word. All we need to do is to get both Phoenix and JaMichael on the same page. We do that, and we can all be eating good. Sometimes, it ain't all about the bloodshed." Makaroni tried to calm down. Sometimes, Stevo got him so riled up that it drove him crazy.

"Nigga, it's always about the bloodshed. That's the only way younger people will listen. But I guess we'll figure that out later. Anyway, I've heard you out loud and clear, Rubio. It was a pleasure." Stevo already had his mind made up. He was traveling to Memphis to kill both JaMichael and Phoenix. He figured with them out of the picture, that he could be making twice as much money as he was currently making. He was all for it.

Rubio stood up and extended his hand. "I'll be in touch. Hopefully, we all will have an understanding before or on Sunday."

"You can look forward to hearing from me before Sunday. Believe that." He shook his hand, and eyed Makaroni.

Makaroni rose. He shook Rubio's hand. "I appreciate your patience. I assure you that we will figure this thing out in time. You have my word on that."

Rubio nodded. "I hope so."

Ghost

Chapter 13

When Makaroni got back to Milwaukee, he got a text from Montana, telling him to come to her place immediately. She said that it was urgent. He pulled in front of her at two in the morning. She opened the door with bare feet, and in a short robe. He stepped past her. "Shorty, what's good? Why you needed me to get over here so fast?"

Montana rubbed her eyes with her fists. "Boy, give me a second. I just woke up." She closed the door.

Makaroni took a seat on her sofa. All of the things Rubio Flores had ordered were going through his head so much that he felt like screaming. He had to find a way to bring both JaMichael, and his father, Phoenix together. He already knew that Stevo was planning on killing them both so he could take the easy way out. He honestly couldn't blame him. Neither Phoenix nor JaMichael were any kin to him. Their lives meant nothing to him. Makaroni had to admit that he cared less before he found out that Phoenix was both he and Montana's biological father.

Montana stood in front of him inside of the small living room. It was basically dark with a hint of moonlight shining in through the patio door. "Boy, do you know that Stevo killed Dexter?"

"What? When he do this?" Makaroni asked, jumping up. He didn't really care much about Dexter, but it seemed to him that Stevo was trying to kill Keaira's entire family. He found that weird, and a bit disturbing.

"Yesterday. He tried to kill Kandace again, too. She wound up getting away after he had already shot down Dexter, though. Somethin' is seriously wrong with him."

Makaroni frowned. "Wait a minute. Stevo was in Chicago with me last night. What time did all of this happen yesterday?"

Montana shrugged. "Earlier." She picked up her phone. "Look, it's all over Facebook."

Makaroni saw people gathering around the site where Dexter had been killed. He read the brief report that didn't say much other than Dexter having been shot multiple times. That he was recently released from jail and had multiple felonies on his record. Makaroni didn't understand why that made a difference, but it was what they wrote. He handed Montana back her phone. "That's fucked up."

"It's more than fucked up. That girl done already lost her sister, and possibly her nephew, too. Now her brother gone. How much more can she take?" Montana asked. She turned her back to him. "And what do you mean that both you and Stevo were in Chicago? What? You back kicking it with him again? Even after what he did to me?"

Makaroni shook his head. "N'all, we had some dual business to tend to. That's all. Both of our presences were demanded. Sis, if JaMichael and Phoenix don't get their shit together, they gon' both be killed by the Sinister Cartel. That's if Stevo don't get to them first, though."

"Stevo? What do you mean? You think he finna kill JaMichael, and our father, too? Damn, you are literally letting him get away with murder. When will you step up and shut that shit down?"

Makaroni flared his nostrils. He felt his blood pressure rising. "Montana, I can't solve every fuckin' thing. I wish I could sis, but I can't. Both JaMichael and Phoenix are acting like females over the control of Memphis, and the Rebirth. They need to let that shit go or the both of them will be murdered by Rubio Flores."

Montana had heard of Rubio's name and she'd heard nothing but bad things. Jahliya had told her that Rubio had zero tolerance for most Black kingpins that ran under his regime. She'd said the fact that he had not killed or put the hit out on JaMichael, and Phoenix this far, was a blessing within itself. "So, what are you going to do, Makaroni?"

"I don't know yet. This shit got me so stressed out. I'm losing my mind." He rubbed his temples. "Where is Kandace?"

"She took some sleep medicine and laid it down. But come here. Don't think about none of that right now. Just hug me for a minute. You need to draw some of my strength away from me." She wrapped her arms around him.

Makaroni melted into her. Her perfume rose into his nostrils. "I think I need you, sis. My mind fucked up right now, and it's the only one way I know I can unclog it." He held her head up until he could look into her eyes.

"But I thought you wasn't getting down on that level with me no more because of all the stuff she said." Montana gave him the puppy dog eyes. "I didn't think you were going to want me anymore." She poked out her bottom lip.

Makaroni grabbed it with his own lips and sucked it into his mouth. "I know I'm bogus, but I don't even care. My mind so fucked up right now. I just need to unlock it. Maybe, this can be our last time. What do you think?"

Montana held the sides of his faces and sucked all over his lips. "I don't know, Mack. I guess we'll just have to see." Her tongue wormed into his mouth. She sucked his tongue. "I want you so bad."

Makaroni's hands were already under her robe. He squeezed her ass. He pulled her cheeks apart and rubbed her hot pussy lips while he sucked hard on her neck. "I want you baby. I need our bond. I need us to go where can't nobody else get to us. Deep within our own world." He bit into her neck and picked her up. She wrapped her legs around him. He sat her on the couch and opened her thick thighs wide. He knelt between them and pushed her knees to her chest. Her pussy popped out at him. He kissed the lips softly. He blew on them, and ever so slowly, opened them up. By use of the moonlight, he could see her glistening pink. He took his tongue, and licked up and down her slit. He kissed her jewel, before sucking it into his mouth.

Montana placed both feet on the couch pillows and gave herself to him. She moaned and sucked on her bottom lip. "Mack, it feel so good, baby. It feel so, so good. I missed you. Fuck. I missed you. I thought mama was. Ooo. Shit. Gone. Make. You. Uhhhh. Shit. Stop. Messing wit' me. Unn!" She cocked her thighs further apart.

Makaroni was in a zone. He didn't want to think. His tongue traveled around and around Montana's clit. He sucked on it while his tongue dived in and out of her hole. Her juices drenched his chin. He kept munching and hitting all of the spots that he knew would drive Montana crazy. His tongue stretched as far as it could go inside of her. His nose rubbed back and forth against her pleasure button. He pulled his tongue out, and sucked her clit again.

Montana screamed, and came hard. She shook for a full minute while Makaroni continued to lick all over her. After the shaking stopped, she pushed him back and laid him on the floor. In seconds, his dick was out, and in her mouth. She sucked him hungrily with her ass in the air. Makaroni rubbed all over it. He slid his middle finger into her as deep as it could go. He pulled it out and added a second one. He ran them in and out. Montana brought her mouth from his dick and moaned at the top of her lungs.

Kandace was shocked as she watched the pair in action. She couldn't believe her eyes. Montana's loud moans had awakened her out of her short slumber. She didn't know what to do as she watched them, or what to think. She tried to divert her mind from what had taken place with her brother. She didn't want to dwell on it. She wanted to be lost in the moment.

Makaroni laid on his back and pulled Montana on top of him. She held his piece, then slid her hot wet kitty down on his pole. He groaned at feeling her. "Damn, girl. This pussy so good."

Montana held his chest. Her knees were placed on each side of him. She started to ride him slow at first, and gradually built up speed. "Unn. Unn. Unn. Mack. Baby. Shit. Fuck me." She rode faster with her mouth wide open.

Makaroni rubbed all over her jiggling ass. His fingers searched her crease from the back. He felt his pole lodged deep inside of her. They were sticky where their sexes connected. He bounced her up and down at full speed. Her titties worked themselves out of her robe. Both nipples peaked. Makaroni rolled her on to her back and got to killing her pussy. "Take this dick. Take this dick. Gimme that pussy. Give it to meeee-ah!" He started to cum back to back inside of her.

"Un-un! No you don't! No. You don't!" She pulled his dick out of her and got on to her knees. She sucked him back into her mouth, working her head into his lap. She could taste their blended juices. She could taste his cum, and it drove her crazy. She squeezed his pipe as hard as she could to bring more of his seed out of him. As she sucked, he became harder and harder. When he was back to full mass, she hopped on top of him. She slid him back into her body and fucked him as fast and as hard as she could while he pulled her down so he could suck her breasts.

"Uhhhh, Mack! Mack! I. Love you! I love you!" She screamed, slamming her box down on him again and again. "I love you baby!"

Makaroni mumbled his love back to her. He was lost. Her pussy felt so good that he couldn't stop his eyes from rolling into the back of his head. He groaned.

Kandace came into the room with her hand inside of her panties. She stopped halfway and knelt a few feet away from them. She could feel the heat of their bodies from the short distance. She could smell their rawness. It drew her closer. She felt like it had been an eternity since anyone had touched her. She needed it. She wanted to be touched so she couldn't dwell on the fact that she'd lost her brother only hours prior. Her fingers ran up and down her slippery lips. She moaned deep within her throat.

Montana rolled her hips. She'd cock as far back as the tip of Makaroni's dick head, before she slammed forward as hard as she could. She felt him dig deeply into her center. It sent ripples of sexual euphoria throughout her body. She dug her nails into his shoulder blades, and bounced higher, only to come down harder, over and over.

Makaroni rose from the carpet to dig as deep as he could. His lap was soaking wet. He pulled Montana down to him, and kissed all over her neck and face. His tongue trailed to her lips. They tongued each other down passionately, breathing heavy, and gasping with each bite of teeth. Montana licked all over his neck. She fucked him faster and harder. Makaroni shuddered while holding her. Her big juicy booty jiggled like crazy. He dug his nails into her, and sat up to bite her neck. "Montana, I'm finna cum. I'm finna cum, baby." He flipped her over, and proceeded to pound her out from the missionary position. From this angle, he could watch her breasts bounce up and down. The sight was so erotic. So wrong. So needed.. Then, he slammed home fifteen hard times, giving her all of him. "Arrrrghh, fuck! I'm cumming. I'm cumming!" He leaned down, and continued to stroke her for all she was worth.

Montana felt his jets hitting her walls, and started to scream. His piece jumped inside of her, spilling its fluids. It was her turn for her eyes to roll into the back of her head. She screamed, and came harder than she ever had before while Makaroni continued to pound her out.

Kandace was working herself over like crazy. Her panties were beside her. Her thighs wide open. Her fingers plunged deep inside of her box repeatedly. She was so wet that she made sound effects. She humped her butt up from the carpet. She watched Makaroni pull out of Montana. She saw the length of his piece in its shiny, wet, glory. The sight was enough to send her over the edge. She imagined him fucking her like he done Montana and it was too much. She moaned out loud, and came while thumbing her clit.

Makaroni was the first to hear the noise, and react to it. He slid his hand under the couch, and grabbed his .40 Glock he'd placed there. He turned around to find Kandace pulling her panties up. She jogged back down the hallway and closed the guestroom door, embarrassed. Montana came over to him and kissed his lips. "It's good, bruh. She was just a lil' horny. She got to see a show. Hopefully, it'll help her get some sleep now." She licked Makaroni's lips, and squeezed his dick. Her insides were still quivering.

He rubbed between her legs. Juices seeped on to his fingers, and dripped off. "Thank you, Montana. On some real shit, I needed that." He kissed her forehead.

"It's all good. We in this shit together. I don't care what we gotta do to get through it. As long as we are together, we will. I truly believe that. Our bond is our strength. It always will be. Come on, let's go get some sleep for a few hours. We done already fucked. I need you to hold me. Show *me* how much you love me. That too much to ask?"

Makaroni laughed. "For you, I'd give up the world, girl. Let's get some sleep." Makaroni hoped that Kandace was okay. He wanted to check in on her, but now that she had caught he and Montana in the act, he felt that it would be awkward.

Chapter 14

It was early the next morning. Stevo felt the bed move, in which he was sleeping. Jada sat up and crawled on top of him. She straddled his waist, and placed a knee on each side of him. She grabbed his gun from under his pillow, and cocked it. She pressed the barrel to his forehead with tears running down her cheeks. "Wake up, Stevo. Wake yo punk butt up, you jerk!" She shouted.

Stevo slowly opened his eyes. It was time for him to feed his system with a few lines of the Rebirth. He felt weak, and sick as if he had the flu. It took a second for Jada to zoom into focus. When she did, he saw her crying face, and the gun in her hand. He came on high alert. Fuck. He thought. This bitch got my Glock. "Sis, what's going on? Why you pointing a gun at me?" He questioned.

Jada had her mind made up. Stevo ruined her life. She needed to kill him. She needed to get her life back, and she felt the only way that she could, was if she took his life away from him. "You did this to me. You ruined my life, Stevo. They just sent me an email from school telling me that I missed two of my most important exams. I can't make them up. My life is ruined. You did this to me!" She screamed. She steadied the gun.

"Whoa, Bitch. Now, calm yo ass down. Let's talk about this shit here." He held his hands out where she could see them. The only thing going through his mind was survival. He loved Jada, but nowhere as near as much as he loved himself. He needed to disarm her without it costing him his precious life. "Jada, I love you sis. I'm sorry about the email. I'm sorry about the exams, sis. But listen to me, you don't need to kill me over this. I love you, girl."

Jada clenched her teeth. "You don't love me, Stevo. You don't love nobody but your got damn self. You dropped into my life, and you ruined it. You've taken me to hell. I hate you so much." She cried. She wiped away her tears. She didn't think he deserved the satisfaction of seeing her cry. No man did, but especially not him.

Stevo couldn't help but to fixate on the fact that she said she hated him. The words were like a blow directly to his heart. "You hate me, Jada? Really? Your only fuckin' brother?"

"Yes! I hate your fuckin' guts. You are the Devil! You are nothing but evil, Stevo. Now, I gotta kill you. It's the only way for me to get my life back." She opened her eyes wide, and sniffed snot back into her nose. She was trying to muster up the courage to do what she knew she needed to do. She didn't understand how people could kill so easily. As much as she hated Stevo, whenever she thought about pulling the trigger, it terrified her. She didn't know what would come after that.

Stevo started to grow angry. "You gon' kill me, sis? Huh, Bitch? I'm supposed to be yo' mafuckin' brother and this how you finna do me? Huh? Well, you know what, kill me then, Jada. Gone head on. Pull the fuckin' trigger right now. Do it!" He was praying that she didn't. He was hoping that the orders had a reverse effect on her.

Jada shook her head. "Aw, I can't. Damn you, Stevo. I'm not a fuckin' murderer like you probably are." He took the gun away from her, and placed it on the bed beside them. She covered her face with her hands.

Stevo pulled her down to him. He flipped her on to her back, and straddled her. He was so mad that he didn't know what he was going to do to her. Had it been anybody else, he would've murdered them immediately.

"Let me go, Stevo! Get off of me!" She yelled. She struggled against him.

"Listen to me, Jada. I love you, bitch. I swear I do. But if you ever put another muthafuckin' gun to my head, I'ma be forced to handle my business on yo ass. You understand me, lil' mama?"

She stopped fighting him. "You know what, Stevo, just do it. Kill me. My life is already over. Fuckin' kill me, Stevo I don't even care anymore!" She screamed.

He continued to hold her down. He looked into her beautiful face. There was no way that he could hurt her any further. There was no way that he could ever kill Jada. He didn't think that he had that savage bone in his body to do anything like that to her. He loved her way too much. "I love you, lil' girl." He smiled.

She looked up at him with hatred. "Don't call me no fuckin' lil' girl. I'm a grown woman."

"I don't care what you is. You're my baby sister." He kissed her lips, and sat back. "You hate me fa real, though?"

She glared at him. "Ever since you came into my life, there has been nothing but bad things happening. You are Satan. I just know it."

Stevo hopped out of the bed, and grabbed his gun. He wore nothing but boxers. His muscular chest, and eight pack abs made him look like an action figure. "I might be Satan to everybody else sis, but not to you. I seriously love you. I mean that."

Jada slipped out of the bed, and stood up. She wore a tank top that came to the top of her thigh gap with nothing underneath it. The room was so hot that both of them were sweating. "How could you love me when you got me hooked on your poison? I'm sick every other hour because of you. That's not love. No way, no how."

Stevo pulled a syringe out of the top dresser drawer, filled with the Rebirth. He flicked his nail against it. "So, what are you saying? You saying you don't want no more of this. Is that it?" Stevo teased.

Jada felt her inside contract. She imagined pumping the drug into her system, and shuddered. "You know that I can't say no to that shit as much as I want to. Why are you doing this to me?"

"Doing what? I'm standing over here minding my own business. What's it been, though? About eight hours since you had a fix? You bout ready, huh?" He pulled the plastic top off of the syringe, and squirted some of the drug into the air. It came down, and stained the white carpet." This is all of the Rebirth that I got left until I go pick up another shipment." He lied. He squirt more of it into the air.

Jada wanted to kill him for real now. "Are you out of your fuckin' mind?" She hollered looking over the stains on the carpet. She glanced to see the syringe only three quarters full. A migraine kicked in full bore. Her vision began to go cloudy. "Stevo, please give it to me. I need it."

Stevo backed away from her. "Why would I give you my last when you done already admitted to hating me? What type of an idiot would that make me?"

Jada didn't want to go through this. She didn't want to beg him. She already hated his guts. Now, she was wishing that she would have killed him. "Stevo, you said you loved me, right?" She walked up to him.

"Yeah, what about it?" He gave her a knowing look.

"Well, if you love me, you wouldn't let me go through all of this pain. I'm sick. I need that syringe. Please. I am begging you." She held her stomach and fell to her knees. The shirt rose and flashed her mound to his eyes.

Stevo felt bad for playing with her like he was. He sighed, and tossed the syringe to her. "Huh, sis. That's my bad."

She caught it. She got up and sat on the bed. In a matter of minutes, the Rebirth was in her system. She laid back on the bed with her thighs wide open. Her tongue licked around her lips. She rubbed her sex, and closed her eyes.

Stevo needed out of the room, just as there was a knock on Jada's front door.

***

Barron balled up his fingers and beat on Jada's door again. He tried to peek into her front window but it was covered by a curtain. "Jada! Jada!" More beating. "Open up." He ordered. Jada hadn't been answering his calls or texts. She had been completely ignoring him and he refused to stand for it. He beat on the door again.

Stevo pulled the door open, and mugged Barron with hatred. "What the fuck you doing beating on my sister door like that for, homey? You think you own her or somethin'?" Stevo snapped.

Barron looked him up and down. He dismissed him, and brushed past him. "Where is Jada? Jada? Baby, where are you?" He hollered. He ran down the hallway to her bedroom, and pushed open the door. Jada was laying on the bed with her thighs splayed wide. Her eyes were closed. She was in another world. "Jada, baby. Why haven't you answered my calls?" Barron shouted.

Jada sat up. Her vision blurry. "Barron, is that you?"

Barron knelt beside her. He could tell immediately that something wasn't right. He rubbed her face. "Baby, what's the matter? What are you on?"

Jada made out his face clearly now. "Barron? Hey baby, I missed you so much." She slurred. "I'ma be back to school in a few days. I'm studying." She lied. Then, she nodded out.

Stevo stepped into the room. "Boy, if you don't get yo sucka ass out my sister shit, I'm finna get reparations out yo ass right now." He balled his fists.

Barron hopped up. "What did you do to her, you son of a bitch?" He walked toward Stevo with a mug on his face.

Stevo stood his ground. "You got until the count of ten to get yo pink ass up out my sister shit. If I get to ten and you ain't gone, we about to have a serious problem."

"You think I'm afraid of you because you're some hippidy hop gangster wannabe from the hood, my man. Do ya? Well, if you do, then you have me sadly mistaken. I'm not afraid of you." He stepped closer to Stevo.

"One. Two. Three." Stevo began to count.

Jada came out of her nod. "Barron, where are you? Barron!" She hollered.

Barron rushed to her side. He knelt down again. "I'm right here, babe. Come on, I'm getting you out if here this instant." He tried to pull her up.

Stevo stepped next to him. "Five. Six. Seven."

"What the fuck is your problem, dude? You can count all you want but I am not worried about you or whoever you think you are. I love her, and she's coming with me. You can continue to count once we are out of here." He pulled Jada up by the arm. "Come on, babe."

"Eight. Nine." Stevo grabbed a silver baseball bat from Jada's closet. He inched closer to the pair. He cocked back the baseball bat ready to swing. "Ten!"

Barron looked up just in time. He jumped back, and the bat came whooshing past his face to slam Jada in the right shoulder. She was so high that she couldn't even feel it. She fell to the floor, dizzy and enwrapped within the euphoric clutches of the Rebirth. She closed her eyes, and curled into a ball on her side. Now, she wanted to be left alone. Barron looked down on her with anger. "Now, you've done it." He ran full speed, and tackled Stevo into the dresser of Jada's room. *Whoom!* His back crashed hard. Stevo kept his grip on the back while he hollered out in pain. Barron took a step back and blazed him with a right cross, and then a left hook, knocking blood from Stevo's mouth. Stevo fell to the carpet next to Jada.

"Get up, you son of a bitch. I'm not afraid of you. You can't do a drive by on me. We're already in the fuckin' house!" Barron grabbed Stevo's ankle and pulled as hard as he could.

Stevo felt the blood drip from his busted lip all the way down the side of his neck. He grew furious. He swung and connected the bat to the side of Barron's face. *Bam!*

Barron fell backward onto his ass. Stevo jumped up. Barron did as well. Barron rushed him with his head down. "Arrgh!" He grabbed Stevo around the waist and picked him up into the air. He slammed him on his back, and kicked him in the stomach. Stevo rolled on to his side with the wind knocked out of him. He struggled to breathe.

Barron was a star hockey player. He had been hit with a hockey stick many times. While the bat hurt him, it did very little to knock him off of his square. He stood over Stevo. "Get up. Get your shit, and get the fuck out of here. Scram loser!"

Stevo felt horrible. His back continued to lock up with every move that he made. He groaned in pain. "You bitch ass nigga. You got me. You got me real good." He staggered to the doorway.

"Don't call me a nigger, you fuckin' loser. White boys can't be that, only you can. Now, get!" He pointed toward the door.

Stevo nodded. He held his ribs while he made his way through the bedroom door, and into the hallway. "I got you, bitch. I swear I do."

"Yeah, yeah." Barron closed the door behind him, and ran to Jada's side. She still had her eyes closed. He knelt, and tapped her cheek. "Come on, baby. I'm going to get you out of here." He slowly pulled her up. They stood up. Barron looked down and saw that Jada's privates were exposed. "I can't take you out like this. Let's find you some pants." He guided her to the bed where she sat.

Jada ran her hand over her face. She smacked her lips. A loud melodious tune played loudly in her head. She smiled, and swayed from right to left with her eyes closed. She scratched her inner forearm so much that it bled. When she opened her eyes to see what she had done, she wanted to scream.

Stevo crept back into the room with his silenced .40 Glock leading the way. His face was a mask of fury. He felt emasculated after getting his ass handed to him. He stepped all the way into the room. "Say nigga?"

Barron turned to face him. He was already prepared to kick his ass again. "What? Aw, shit."

"Aw, shit is right." Stevo aimed and shot him through both of his knees simultaneously.

Barron buckled, and fell to the floor. His kneecaps blew off behind him. He wound up on his side groaning. "You motherfucker. Aww. You son of a bitch. I'm going to kill you."

Stevo replaced his gun. He picked the baseball bat up off of the floor. "Now, where were we?" He laughed.

"What's your problem? Just leave here. Please!" Barron hollered.

It was too late. Stevo rushed him with the baseball bat, and beat him senselessly until his arms gave out. He took a short breath, and beat him some more. When it was all said and done, he beat him to death with no mercy. The bedroom was splattered with Barron's blood. It dripped from the ceiling. Ran down the walls, and covered the carpet.

Jada hugged her knees and rocked back and forward. The Rebirth was still running rampant in her system. "Why, Stevo? Why? Why would you do that?" She cried.

Stevo sat beside her, and hugged her to his chest. "There, there, lil' sis. It's just us now. We don't need nobody else." He kissed her cheek, and stood up. "I gotta get rid of this fool. I'll be back."

Ghost

Chapter 15

Maisey grabbed two big grocery bags out of the trunk of her car, and slammed it shut. She took a glance into the interior of the car and made sure that she hadn't left anything inside of her car, before she made it up the steps to her home. It was three o'clock in the afternoon, and she was already tired. She wanted to get inside, put the few groceries away, and take her a quick nap before she had to get up and cook.

She fit the key into the lock, and found it odd when there was no need to turn it. Her door opened. She became alarmed. She sat the bags down on the porch, and stepped into her home. "Hello, is anybody in here?" She asked inching further and further inside. There was silence. She came all the way inside of the house and continued to walk as slow as she could. Her antennas were all the way up. She eased out of the front room.

"Hello? Anybody here?" She kept going. When she got into the living room, she stopped in place. Cassidy sat tied to a chair. Her mouth, and eyes duct taped. "Shit." Maisey turned around to run. Before she could get all the way around, she bumped into Seth's big chest. He stood still. His eyes were big as snowballs. He breathed heavy. There was a .9 millimeter in his right hand. Maisey backed up, and held up her hands. "Look, Seth. I don't know what you got going on with my homegirl, but you know what, y'all are married. The Bible says that we are supposed to leave the marital bed undefiled. I ain't got no other choice than to leave you two to y'all own business. I'm out of here." She attempted to walk toward the back door.

Seth raised the gun. "Maisey, if you move, I am going to shoot you." He promised. His voice was low, and authoritative.

Maisey froze in her tracks. "What do you want from me, Seth? I don't have anything to do with what's going on between you and your wife. Please, just let me leave out of here. I ain't seen nothin', and I won't say nothin'."

Seth yanked her by the shoulder until she was facing him. He placed the gun in her face. "Did you know?"

Maisey swallowed her spit. She was scared for her life. She could smell the heavy odor of alcohol coming off of Seth. She sensed that he wasn't in his right state of mind. She could only imagine the extent he'd go over his and Cassidy's failed marriage.

"Did you know?" He hollered.

"Did I know what?" Maisey was beginning to freak out.

"Did you know that she was sleeping with Makaroni?"

Maisey shook her head. "That's my son. Had I known anything like that was going on, I would have put a stop to it right away. That's my baby. What else is a mother supposed to do?"

Seth held the gun out. "I don't believe you, Maisey. I think that you and this whore of Babylon played me for a fool. You knew that she was cheating on me the whole time. Admit it!"

Maisey backed up with her hands shoulder length. "Seth, I swear I didn't. I would've never allowed for any of that to go on. You should know me better than that." She scolded.

Seth grabbed her by the blouse. He yanked her toward the living room table. "Sit down, Maisey! Now!"

Maisey took a seat next to a squirming Cassidy. Cassidy screamed with the duct tape around her mouth. Maisey felt sorry for her. She could see hints of the black eyes that Seth had obviously given her. The duct tape didn't cover all of her injuries.

Seth picked up the duct tape from the table. "Tape your mouth. Do it. Hurry up!" He yelled.

Maisey rolled the duct tape around until she could find the seam of where she could pull off a new piece. When she did, she pulled on it. "I ain't got nothing to do with this, Seth. You need to let me go. You know that it's the right thing to do."

"Fuck the right thing. I got something special planned for the both of you whores. You betta believe that. Now, pull a piece off and put it over your eyes. Now!"

Maisey felt her heart pounding in her chest. Something told her that if she put that tape over her eyes, that she would never see the light of day again. She could tell that Seth was scarred. He wanted revenge in the worst way. She had to buy time. She didn't know for what, but she needed it. "Seth, just get even with me."

Seth paused. "What?" He was confused. The liquor had him slightly out of his mind.

"I said just get even with me. She slept with Makaroni behind your back, and it crushed you. How about you sleep with me in front of her, and then you guys will be even. Nobody has to die here today, Seth. Besides, for you and I, it would be long overdue." She batted her eyelashes as much as she could under the circumstances, and ran her tongue over her lips.

Seth looked her over. Her blouse was slightly opened. He could make out her cleavage. Both cinnamon colored mounds appealed to the sexual animal inside of him. Maisey was a beautiful woman. Far more gorgeous than Cassidy. He'd always felt that way. She wasn't known for sleeping with a barrage of men. She carried herself like a true queen. This fact is what did it for Seth. "You would be willing to do that, Maisey?"

She nodded. "I've always found you so damn handsome, Seth. I've wanted you for years." She lied, feeding into his ego. "You think I let y'all move up in here because of Cassidy? Boy, please. This whole time, I was hoping that you made a move on me. You just never did. Had you did, I would've went in a heartbeat."

He smiled. The alcohol caused his common sense to lack. He imagined all of the times he'd seen Maisey in the house wearing next to nothing. Her body was so gorgeous to him. He had never seen a finer woman in person. He truly felt that way. "Stand up, Maisey.

Maisey stood. She dropped the tape on the table. "I'm up, Seth. Now what?"

Seth hesitated in giving her an order. "Open your blouse for me."

Maisey untucked her blouse. She slowly unbuttoned it from the bottom up. She looked into his eyes the entire time. When all of the buttons were undone, she pulled opened the blouse. "Now what?"

Seth saw the swells of her breasts, and became erect. The beats of his heart sped up. "Take that bra off."

Maisey unhooked her bra from the front, and allowed her twin beauties to fall out of their cups. She dropped the bra to the carpet, and cuffed her breasts. She felt nervous. She was looking for any weakness in him. If she saw any room to attack him, she was going for it. "Anything else?"

Seth was so excited that he could barely breathe. "Take your hands away. Let me see them."

Maisey held them a bit longer. She knew how to tease a man. The more you kept them waiting, the more they lost themselves. "Seth, I wanna hear you tell me to take my hands away again."

"P-P-Please take your hands away." He stuttered.

Maisey smiled. She dropped her firsthand, exposing her right breast. Then, she dropped the left one. She stood there in all of her glory. "Do you like them?"

Seth had forgot why he had come to Maisey's home to begin with. He stared at her with lust in his heart. "They are absolutely beautiful. The most perfect pair I have ever seen in my entire life." He admitted.

Cassidy felt a twinge of jealousy. She couldn't believe that he had said that. She wondered if he actually felt that way, or if he was simply living in the moment. He was drunk. She reasoned. Though, she had to admit, Maisey's big nippled breasts were stunning.

"Well, what do you want to do with them, Seth? Come on, you can tell me?" She flirted.

Seth stepped closer. "Can I touch them?"

Maisey looked him over. "Sure baby."

Seth got closer. He held the gun with his right hand. He reached with his left, and squeezed her breasts one at a time. Their heat felt amazing to him. He ran his thumb around her nipples until they were erect. He pinched them, and shivered. She felt disgusted by his touch. For her, it was reminiscent of Stacy. But Seth wanted more. "Take those pants off, Maisey. I wanna see all of you. "

She cringed. "Okay, Seth. Long as you can promise me that you ain't gon' hurt nobody." She attempted a weak laugh. It sounded more like a nervous giggle.

"Take them off." He ordered. He was feening to see Maisey in the buff. Her body was so righteous to him with the clothes on, he could only imagine what she looked like with them off. "Hurry up."

Maisey unbuttoned her Jordache jeans, and pulled them down. Her purple bikini panties came into view first. The material all up in her crease. She bent over, and pulled them all the way down and off. She stood before him in just her panties. "There we go."

Seth felt like he was about to pass out. The thought of sleeping with Maisey had crossed his mind so many times, but never once did he believe that he stood a chance. But to see her standing before him in next to nothing, was slowly beginning to drive him insane. He stepped up and rubbed the material of her panties. Gradually, his hand ventured between her thighs. He rubbed the crotch, and felt the heat radiating from her pussy.

"Damn, Maisey, you sure you'd let me have some of this? It sure would make things right. I can tell you that right now." He cuffed her mounds, and imagined what it would feel like to be inside of her. Cassidy being present made things all the more better for him. She deserved to watch him get even after what she'd done with Makaroni.

"Seth, if it will ensure that nobody gets hurt tonight, then I'm all for it. You just have to promise me that you will put that gun away. We can squash all of this by you and I laying down together."

Seth rubbed her stomach, and slipped his hand into her waistband, trailing his fingers downward until he found her hidden lips. He rubbed over them, and looked into Maisey's eyes. "You got a deal." He continued to rub her while placing the gun into the small of his back.

Maisey felt sick. She'd never found Seth attractive. He reminded her too much of Howard. They were the same height, and weight. They laughed alike, and even wore the same cologne. Her heart was blackened toward Howard. She didn't need any reminders of him, especially not when it came to anything sexual. She prayed that Seth gave her an opening to take advantage of the situation. She didn't think she could live with herself if he entered her body. It would take her years to get over it. She was sure of that. "Where do you want to do this?" She asked.

He ran his fingers up and down her slit, hesitant to penetrate her. He still couldn't believe that it was real. He slowly pulled his hand, and rubbed his fingers together. Maisey was naturally juicy. He shivered, and looked over at Cassidy. He sucked his fingers into his mouth, savoring the flavor of Maisey. "We gon' do this shit right here in front of her. I had to watch her with Makaroni, so she gotta watch me with you. That's how it has to go."

Maisey nodded in understanding. "Okay, baby. That's cool." She stepped up to him, and slid her arms around his neck. Her nose touched his. She closed her eyes, and turned her head to the side. She kissed his lips.

Seth groaned. He held her waist, and returned her kiss with as much passion as he could muster. He was so excited. This was Maisey. She had been the finest girl in their High School. He'd had a crush on her, even before he was married. His tongue slipped into her mouth. He sucked all over her lips, and dared to grab her ass.

Maisey felt like she was getting ready to throw up. She could taste the Jack Daniels mixed with his breath. She gagged and hoped that he didn't catch on to her being disgusted. She pulled her head back, and smiled.

Seth had his eyes closed. He was still making the kissing movements with his lips when she pulled back to look at him. He looked pathetic. She stepped forward again, and rubbed all over his muscular back. He continued to kiss all over her. Her stomach turned when he licked both of her lips. He sucked the top one into his mouth, and kept it before letting it go. Maisey rubbed on his lower back. "Mmm, Seth I've been waiting for this moment with you for years." She lied.

Seth grabbed her ass. He took the waistband of the panties and pulled them down to her ankles. "Well, you finna get your chance right here, and now. I've been yearning for you, too. Lift your foot."

Maisey reluctantly lifted her right foot, then her left. She watched him take her panties and sniff the crotch. The act disgusted her further. "You like how I smell baby?"

Seth nodded. "Hell yeah. Come here, Foxy Mama." He pulled her to him, and sucked all over her neck. His hands opened her cheeks. He cuffed them, and grew hard. He slipped his right hand down the middle of them so he could play with her some more. "I'm ready, Maisey. I'm ready to fuck this cat."

Maisey began to panic. She wasn't ready. She didn't want him to touch her anymore. There was no way she could give him her body and not want to kill herself directly afterward. She still hadn't found her opening to grab the gun. "Seth, maybe we should do this in the bedroom." She blurted out. She didn't know what she was saying. She was hoping to buy some time.

Seth shook his head. "N'all, baby. We finna do this shit right here, and right now. I want Cassidy to experience this. Maybe afterwards she will start to appreciate me a little more. So lay down, and give me what I got coming."

Chapter 16

"Okay, Seth." Maisey took a deep breath, and looked into Cassidy's eyes. She felt sick. She couldn't believe she was about to endure what she had never wanted to. She hated men so much. They were always so sexual. She wished men dived into their emotions. It would have saved the world a whole lot of turmoil. She reasoned. She lowered herself to her back on the carpet. She spaced her knees. "Come on, Seth."

Seth couldn't believe the sight before him. He looked between Maisey's thighs and wanted to jump up and kick his heels together. He was so close. He knelt between them, and pulled his piece through his zipper. He stroked it. "I been waiting for this moment ever since I met yo' fine ass." He went into a push up position.

Cassidy rocked her chair as hard as she could. She couldn't allow for Maisey to be her sacrifice. She couldn't let her bite the bullet. She knew how she secretly felt about Seth. She knew she hated him. She rocked the chair with all of her strength until it fell over next to them. She screamed in the duct tape.

Seth jumped back. "What the fuck?" He climbed from between Maisey's thighs, and grabbed ahold of Cassidy. "Bitch, what is wrong with you? You done cheated with that boy. Now, it's my turn." He started to pick her up.

Maisey saw her chance to grab ahold of the gun that was tucked into his lower back. She sat up, and grabbed the handle. "Give me this!"

Before she could reach it, Seth backhanded her so hard that she went flying back, and the gun slid across the carpet to the left of her. Seth stood up to search for it and immediately spotted it. "I see what you bitches on. And it ain't gon' work."

Maisey jumped up naked, and rushed him. She dove and tackled him into the dining room table, knocking it over. They fell to the floor, tussling. Seth cocked his head back, slamming into her face, busting her nose. Maisey hollered out in pain. She grabbed the back of his neck, and pulled him forward. She bit into his cheek and shook it like a Pitbull.

"Arghhhh" He yelped.

He tried to pry her from his cheek by delivering blows to her jaw repeatedly. Maisey refused to let go. Seth elbowed her in the stomach, knocking the wind out of her. Maisey released him. Seth crawled away from her with blood dripping down his face. He touched it with his right hand and looked his fingers over. Confirming the presence of blood only further freaked him out. Before he could think what to do next, Maisey dove on him, swinging blow after blow. Her fists connecting to his face. The punches were so hard that the slapping of skin resonated all through the house. She gave him a hard right hook, and bit into his face again, shaking it. She could taste his blood on her tongue, but dismissed it.

"Ahhhh! Ahh! Let it go! Let it go!" He elbowed her again knocking her away. She flew backward. He roared and straddled her. He held her down and gave her four hard punches of his own. Blood spurt across the carpet.

Maisey twisted him off of her. She pounced on him from her knees. She landed on top of him swinging for her life. "Get out of my house, Seth. I hate you!"

Cassidy hollered into her duct tape. When the chair had fallen over, one of the handles that her left wrist was taped to, had broken. She wiggled it in a haste. She had to help her best friend. She needed to get to the gun. She did all that she could to break free.

Seth picked Maisey up into the air and slammed her on the table, knocking the wind out of her for the second time. She felt her rib snap. The pain shot through her body. She closed her eyes for a second, and bounced back up. Seth punched her in the jaw, knocking her back down to one knee. Maisey got back up. She staggered on her feet with blood dripping from her mouth. She held up her guards. "Come on. Come on. You finna have to kill me."

Seth spit on the carpet. His face was a mess of bite marks, and blood. He balled up his hands. "This what you want, Maisey? Huh? Alright then. Let's dance." He rushed her swinging like a mad man.

Maisey blocked his first blow, but was hit by the second. Before he could connect the third time, she ducked and uppercut him as hard as she could right on the chin. He grew dizzy. She kicked him in the nuts. He fell back on the table, crashing loud and hard. He jumped right back up with his balls inside of his stomach. Maisey didn't give him no time to gather himself. She was on him. Picking her spots before she landed her blows. She hit his nose, and broke it with a right cross. He hollered out in pain. She swung a left hook and cracked his jaw. Then, spushed him into the wall. He got stuck. She ran to recover this gun and found that Cassidy had broken out of her restraints. She held the gun in her hand. "Gimme the gun, Cassidy. I'm finna kill his ass. Hurry up. Give it to me."

Cassidy backed away from her. "No, girl we can't kill him. He just a little drunk."

Seth struggled to get to his feet. He was in so much pain that tears ran down his cheeks, mixing with the blood that poured out of the chunks of skin that was missing from his face that Maisey had bit away from him. "Don't let that bitch kill me. This ain't my fault." He struggled to get a hold of himself.

Maisey was upset. "Cassidy? What are you waiting for? Give me the gun." She ordered. She held her forearm under her right rib.

Cassidy felt guilty. She was wishing that she had never cheated with Makaroni. She backed away. "Seth, why don't you just leave, baby. I understand you are upset right now. But I think you should leave."

Seth wiped away his blood. "Okay, Cass. I'ma leave. Just give me a hug, baby. Give me somethin' to let me know that you still love me." He held open his arms.

Maisey shook her head as Cassidy slowly walked over to him. "Girl, you're bugging."

"I'm sorry, Seth. I know this is all my fault." She told him. She didn't know why she was having an epiphany all of the sudden, but she was. She knew that they wouldn't have been were they were had she never cheated. She owed Seth more loyalty and respect than what she'd given him. They had been together for a long time. They had been through so much as one. She felt her heart breaking from her betrayals of him. "Just hug me, and get out of here. We'll figure things out at another time. I promise, okay."

Seth nodded. "Okay, baby. Long as you know that I still love you with all of my heart." He opened his arms. Cassidy walked into them. Maisey slowly eased backward out of the room. Seth hugged Cassidy tight with his eyes pinned on Maisey.

When she had backed up too far, something in him snapped. He pushed Cassidy out of his arms, and punched her on the chin, knocking her out before she could hit the ground. The gun fell out of her hand. He bent down and picked it up. He cocked it, and ran at Maisey. "Come here, bitch." He aimed and fired. *Boom!*

He was no longer in his right mind. Maisey saw the kitchen wall explode beside her head. She ran into her bedroom and slammed the door. Her heart pounded in her chest. "Get out of here, Seth. Please!" She locked the door, and ran to the window. She opened it as wide as she could. She slid through it and fell to the ground.

Seth crashed through the bedroom door like a bull. He slung it to the side, and hurried toward the window. He saw Maisey running out of the backyard naked. Her ass jiggled as she booked it through the grass. He aimed and fired. *Boom! Boom! Boom!* "I'ma kill you, bitch." He stuck his head out the window, and fired again. *Boom! Boom!* He cursed, and pulled his head back inside. When he turned around to run out of the bedroom, Cassidy caught him with a steak knife to his chest. His eyes were bucked wide open. He dropped the gun. She moved away from him. He ran toward her, and fell to his knees.

"You made me, Seth. You made me, Seth. You made me do this to you. I didn't want to." She cried.

Seth pulled the knife out of his chest. Blood gushed out of him in a heavy flow like a river. He ran out of the room, and made it into the kitchen where he fell dizzy. His eyesight flashed on and off. His heart began to struggle to beat. His blood pressure dropped considerably low. He felt cold. His cheeks vibrated. He could taste the blood on his tongue.

Cassidy came and stood over him. "I'm sorry, Seth. But you made me do it. You made me do this to you." She fell to her knees beside him.

Seth closed his eyes. He began to shake repeatedly. Blood seeped out of his mouth. "Fuck you, Cassidy." He managed to say. He was dead.

Cassidy covered her face with her hands. She knew it was all her fault. She didn't know how she was going to explain things to Stevo. She didn't know what her next move would be. She cried her eyes out as memories of their relationship over the past twenty years played over in her mind. She had never felt so low in her entire life. She took a final glance at Seth. Blood pooled around his body. The floodgates for her tears broke down her face. She felt weak, still in disbelief that all of it had taken place.

***

Later that night, once Makaroni got word of the incident, he came to clean up the mess. He dumped Seth into the big metal garbage can in the back of the deserted old aluminum factory, dropping a match inside of it. Seth's body engulfed in flames. He took a step back and placed his arm around Maisey's shoulder. He pulled her more protectively to him. "That nigga lucky Cassidy got a hold of him before I had the chance to. I swear to God I would have fucked him over, mama."

Maisey watched Montana step up to the big metal garbage can and pour more gasoline into it. The flames shot ten feet high. Maisey could feel the heat from it warming her. "Boy, watch yo' mouth. I know you're angry but you still gotta give me my due." She stepped toward the garbage can, and stopped. "He got what he deserved. I'm just glad that she took care of him because with her is where it all started. She should've never stepped out on that man. Especially, not with you. She brought that drama to my doorstep. You assisted her, but it's too late to cry over spilled milk. He's gone, and that's just that." She held her ribs as a jolt of pain shot through her.

Makaroni knew he was in the wrong but he couldn't get over the fact that somebody had put their hands on his mother again. Every time the imagery of Seth touching Maisey in anyway came across his mind, he got so angry he started to shake. He really couldn't believe that the man had shot at her. If one of the bullets had connected and taken Maisey away, Makaroni really didn't know how he would've dealt with that.

Montana walked over to Maisey and hugged her. "It's time we get you up out of Milwaukee, mama. It seems like every time we leave you alone for a few seconds, somethin' bad happens. You are all that we have in this world besides each other. We have to protect you. Don't you understand that?" She kissed Maisey's cheek, and hugged her tighter.

"I know, baby. We are all that we have."

"Yeah well, that's why I gotta get some things in order. I got a couple more moves to bust, and then we can say goodbye to Milwaukee for forever. I mean that. This city ain't been nothing but problems for us ever since we got here." He mugged the garbage can with Seth's remains inside of it. He wished he would have been the one that took him off of the face of the earth. "I swear to God, I will never let nothing happen to either one of you again. Y'all getting up out of Milwaukee this week. I'm not playing either."

Maisey stepped away from Montana. "Where the hell are we going to go, Mack? Huh? I ain't got enough money saved up to go nowhere. We have a lot of planning to do before we can go anywhere. Plus, I just got my CNA License. I'm about to start to really make some good money. Leaving Milwaukee ain't an option right now."

"I get what you're saying, Mama." Makaroni started, placing his big hands on her shoulders. "But I ain't trying to hear none of what you're talking about. Don't worry about making no money right now. That license will follow you wherever you go. You earned that. We are leaving this city, and until you can get into your practice wherever we wind up, I'm going to foot the bill for everything. I got a nice amount of chips stacked up. It's all good."

Maisey pushed his hands off of her. "Boy, you are my son. What the hell I look like depending on you for anything? Now, I said when I get myself together, then I will be more apt to leave this city. Until then, I ain't going nowhere. That's final. Come on, let's get up out of here. His ass starting to stank." She headed toward Montana's truck.

Makaroni stood looking dumbfounded. He continued to mug the flaming garbage can. He knew he had to get his family out of Milwaukee. It wasn't safe for any of them. He didn't know what was going to take place with Rubio Flores below the border. He wasn't sure how the war between Phoenix and JaMichael would play out, but he feared the worst. He couldn't allow for the drug war to spill over and place his family in harm's way. He had already failed them enough. This had been the second time Maisey had to endure, and escape one of his enemies, or a person trying to hurt her because of what he had done. That was two strikes. He wouldn't allow for her to endure a third.

Montana slipped her arm around his neck. "Boy, you already know how stubborn mama is. She don't wanna leave this city. She's built a life here after so long. You gon' have to be more convincing than that." She kissed his cheek. "Come on. We still gotta get her to a hospital."

Makaroni nodded his head. Once again, he mugged the flames. His heart felt colder. More black. He wondered what his next move should be. The window of trying to decide it was closing. He got until to Sunday. He had to find a way to make everything that his family had endured make sense.

He had to find a way to protect them, and master the Game. He felt so lost and confused. He sighed, and closed the top to the garbage can. He could hear Seth sizzling, and popping. He had already given orders to two of his hittas that when the fire went out they were to scoop up his ashes and dispose of them into Lake Michigan. They watched him from a distance. He gave them a nod before getting into the passenger's seat of Montana's truck. Montana pulled away from the scene.

Ghost

Chapter 17

It was eight o'clock in the morning, the next day. Jada opened her eyes and was immediately met with a fierce migraine. She winced in pain. She sat up and felt nauseous. She covered her month, and scooted out of the bed. She ran as fast as she could to the bathroom, and fell to her knees. She threw open the toilet, and purged her guts. Her sides felt like they were turned inside out.

Stevo heard her puking and coughing. He held a syringe in his right hand filled up with the Rebirth. He smiled. His eyes were low. He was high has a kite. He'd been tooting the Rebirth all morning with Sasha before he sent her to the pharmacy to pick up his asthma pump. "Look, Shorty, I know you still mad about your lil' boyfriend and all of that shit, but you need to come on back home, lil' sis. The Rebirth is calling you. It's been almost twenty four hours. You gotta be near death already." He joked.

Jada spit in the toilet, and wiped her mouth. "I'm never taking that shit again. I'd rather die first. You can't control me, Stevo. You had no right doing what you did to Barron. He loved me, and you hated that." Another wave of nausea came over her. This time, it felt like she was being punched in the stomach by a heavyweight boxer. She squeezed her eyelids together and threw up as much as she could. Then, she sat back on her haunches, sweating profusely.

Stevo was pissed. "You ain't say shit about that nigga putting his hands on me, though. He could have killed me. Would that have made you happy?" He snapped.

Jada glared at him. She hugged her herself. Chill bumps were all over her body. "Why are you in here?"

Stevo knelt beside her. "Look sis, I ain't trying to fight with you. I love you too much for that. Now, I need you to go ahead and take this fix so you can come back home. You can't keep fighting this shit. You're going to keep getting sicker and sicker. That's how this drug was designed."

Jada slowly made her way to her feet. Her eyes were red. There were serious bags under them. Her skin was dry, yet she couldn't stop sweating around the forehead. The migraine got worst every five minutes to the point that she felt like screaming at the top of her lungs. "Stevo, if you don't get out of here, I'm going to make you kick my ass. I'm not taking your fucking drug anymore. You don't own me! I wish I never picked you up and saved your life that day. You have been nothing but a curse to me ever since then." She fell back to her knees. "Why did you kill Barron? Why won't you leave me alone?" She covered her face with her hands, and broke down.

Stevo was so irritated that he wished Barron was still alive so he could kill him in front of Jada. He hated the things that she said to him. He hoped that she was speaking out of anger. But he couldn't be so sure. The sounds of her sobbing was like nails on the chalkboard to him. He disliked hearing his sister cry. It hurt his black heart. He knelt beside her, and pulled her to him. "Sis, I'm sorry man. I didn't mean to hurt you. I'm still trying to figure all of this shit out. I swear to God that I love you with all of my heart."

Jada allowed for him to hold her for a second. She cried as hard as she could. Her head continued to pound. She caught a whiff of Stevo's cologne, and grew even sicker. She pushed him away from her. "Get away from me, Stevo. I hate you." She pushed him over and over but he stood his ground. She was too weak to move him.

Stevo lost it. He grabbed her left arm, and slung her to the bathroom floor. He pulled the left arm all the way out and sat on the bicep. He grabbed the cap off the syringe, and smacked her thick vein that protruded out of her inner fore-arm.

"Get off of me. Stop! Stop! Please!" She hollered.

Stevo slid the needle into her arm, and eased down on the feeder. He pulled it back to draw up a portion of her blood, then he fed it back to her mixed with the Rebirth. Jada moaned at the top of her lungs as the drug shot through her veins and went straight to her brain, down to her heart, and all over her body. She closed her eyes, and smacked her lips. Stevo eased the syringe out of her. He stood up, and looked down on her.

Jada was curled into a ball on the floor. She laid onto her side. "Why do you keep doing this to me? I didn't want your drug. It's too much for me. I can't handle it, Stevo. I can't handle you, either." She closed her eyes as the Rebirth's high started to get stronger and stronger.

Stevo mugged her. She was dressed in a small tee shirt. It had risen up to her stomach exposing her lower half. He imagined Barron seeing her nude body and it made him want to snap out. He hated him. He was deceased and he still hated him. "I only do this shit because I love you. You don't get it though. I can't have you leaving me. I need you, Jada. You're my mafuckin' sister." Stevo's mind was playing tricks on him. Doing so much of the Rebirth had caused for him to lose some of his common sense. He felt that everything that he was doing was normal, and justified because he had spent his entire life looking for Jada. Now that he'd found her, he never wanted to lose her. He felt that the Rebirth was the only way he could keep her trapped until she came around to see things the way that he did. "I don't know why you loved Barron so much anyway."

"He never hurt me like this. All you've done is hurt me." She closed her eyes, and nodded out.

Stevo picked her up, and carried her to her bedroom. He laid her on the bed, and pulled a sheet over her body. The front door opened. He perked up. "Who the fuck is that?" He took his .9 millimeter out of the small of his back.

Sasha came down the hallway smiling. She stopped in the doorway, and mugged Jada's form. "Daddy, I got a surprise for you. You ain't gon' believe who I saw at the pharmacy."

He frowned. "Bitch, what are you talking about now?"

Sasha dismissed his rudeness. "Baby, your mother is here."

"What? Bitch, don't play with me. I know you ain't brought her here." He looked around the room, and began to panic. Jada squirmed on the bed. She kicked the sheets off of her, and opened her thighs wide. Her naked pussy was on full display.

Sasha grew angry. She thought that Jada was trying to entice him on purpose. She hated the woman. She wished that she was out of the picture already. Before she could respond to his question, Cassidy tapped on the door and walked into the room. The first thing she saw was a naked Jada. She zoomed into her face, and her eyes got bucked. She looked up to an angry Stevo. "Baby, you and I need to talk."

Stevo grabbed both her and Sasha. He pushed them out of the room and closed the door. He pulled the sheet over Jada, and kissed her forehead. "Sis, you gotta put this sheet on you for a minute. You gon' cool down in a second." He turned the fan on, and pointed it toward her.

Cassidy opened the door. "That's Jada, isn't it?"

"Cassidy, get out of the fuckin' room. I'm doing something right now. I'll be out there in a minute!"

"I wanna see her. I wanna see my daughter." She whispered. She looked over the driver's license that Sasha had given her from Jada's glove compartment. After reading the name on it, she placed two and two together. She knew that Jada was her very own daughter.

"Cassidy, I'm not playin' wit' you. Get yo ass out of this room or I'm about to blow my top. Sasha, bitch I'm killing you for this shit. You done fucked up for the last time." He swore.

"But daddy, I didn't do nothing. I saw your mother at Walgreen's and she told me that there had been a family emergency. That she needed to see you. I didn't think I was doing anything wrong." She was terrified. She had never seen Stevo at his angriest but he appeared to be just that. She could only imagine what he had in mind to do to her. She eased out of the bedroom.

Cassidy stepped forward. "Stevo, don't be mad at her. She didn't do anything wrong. I practically grabbed ahold of her clothes to make sure that she brought me to you. You need to stop taking your anger out on everybody else, and direct it at the person that you are really mad at." She came closer to him. She looked down at Jada. "She look sick. We gotta get her to a hospital."

Stevo was furious. "Bitch, now you're all concerned about my sister? You wasn't concerned about her when yo thot ass gave her up for adoption. You don't give a fuck about nobody but yo' self." He snapped feeling his temper rise.

Cassidy tried to remain calm. She hadn't come over to argue with her son. She needed to give him the news about Seth, and she wanted to show him some respect by giving it to him in person. "Stevo, you have no idea what you're talking about. I would really appreciate if you gave me a moment to explain to you what took place with your sister. Give me a chance."

"Bitch, for what? Pops already told me how much of a hoe you was back then. Just like you is now. Don't think I'm sleeping on the fact that you fuckin' my nigga either. Pops told me that he caught you fuckin' Makaroni on more than one occasion. Far as I'm concerned, you ain't nothing but a tramp. You stop being my mother a long time ago." He stepped into her face. "Now, bitch, get the fuck out of my sister's house, and gon' about yo business. Don't none of this shit here concern you."

Cassidy lost her cool. She swung and slapped him as hard as she could. It sounded like a whip against naked skin. *Ka-PISH!* Stevo fell backward on to the bed. "Boy! I don't know who you think you are, but you are not going to fix your mouth to talk to me no any kind of way. I am your mother. You will respect me as such!" She hollered.

Sasha watched from the doorway. She was terrified. She couldn't believe that Cassidy dared to put her hands on Stevo. She was sure that things were about to spiral out of control, and that Cassidy was about to meet Satan head on. She braced herself for what was sure to come next.

Stevo stood up and lowered his eyelids. He casually walked to the door and opened it wide. "Cassidy, I'm going to give you a chance to get the fuck out of my sister's house before I lose myself on yo ass. There is nothin' for you here. Neither Jada nor I need you. We got each other. Now leave, bitch."

Jada groaned and rolled out of the bed. She fell on the floor whimpering in pain. Sweat began to come all over her. She curled into a tighter ball. Her teeth chattered. She felt both hot and cold at the same time. "Mommy." She shivered.

Stevo was shocked. "Mommy? Fuck you calling her for?"

Cassidy broke past him and knelt beside Jada. "Baby, what's the matter? Are you okay? Talk to me."

Jada shook harder. "I'm sick, Mama. He put those drugs in me. Now, I'm sick. I feel like I'm about to die." She closed her eyes and stated to cry.

Cassidy stood up. "What did you do to her? Huh?" She pointed her finger in his face.

Stevo felt his blood boiling. He mugged Cassidy. "Cassidy, get yo finger out of my face. This is your last warning."

Cassidy dropped her finger. "Stevo, I don't know what yo sick ass done but I'm taking her and she's leaving with me." She knelt to grab a hold of Jada. "Come on, baby." Cassidy could smell the stench of unwashed body. She wrapped Jada's arm around her neck and began to lift her.

Stevo watched for a full minute getting hotter and hotter. "So, y'all finna leave me? Huh? Y'all finna leave me?"

Cassidy ignored him. She continued to help her daughter come to her feet. When she had her standing upright, they began to make their way to the door. Cassidy stopped. She was angry at Stevo. She didn't know what he had done, but she just felt that it was something sick. She no longer cared about his feelings. "Oh, and for the record, Seth is dead. I don't have time to explain to you how it happened. But he's gone. I had to take care of him." She continued to make her way toward the opening in the doorway. She knew that she'd sounded harsh but she didn't care. She felt that since Stevo didn't are about anybody else's feelings that she didn't need to care about his. "Mama got you now, baby. You ain't gotta worry about his sick ass no more."

Stevo was shaking so bad that his teeth were now chattering. He closed his eyes. He balled his hands into fist. His head rolled around on his neck. He judged their footsteps and could tell that they were in the middle of the hallway. He couldn't allow for Cassidy to take his sister away from him. He couldn't lose Jada. She was all he felt he truly had. He rushed into the hallway and ran in front of them, blocking their path. He yanked Jada away from Cassidy and pushed her as hard as he could. She stumbled and fell over the table, cracking her head on the side of the wall. "Gimme my sister. We don't need you here!"

Chapter 18

Cassidy slowly made her way to her feet with blood running down her face. It took her a while to get her footing. She touched the wound in her forehead. "You're nuts, Stevo. Somethin' is seriously wrong with you."

Stevo led a reluctant Jada back into the bedroom. He eased her into the bed, and pulled the covers back over her. She was so weak that she couldn't stop him. Her body felt as if it belonged to somebody else. Stevo kissed her forehead. "I love you, Jada. You belong to me. We are all we got. Cassidy is a nobody. She ain't our mama. She's a nobody. You hear me?"

Jada could only hear bells ringing in her head. Her heart was beating so fast that she couldn't think straight. She curled into a tighter ball. She prayed the pain would go away.

Stevo kissed her again. "I love you." He grabbed another syringe out of the top dresser drawers and came back to Jada.

Jada opened blurry eyes. A tear ran down her cheek. She felt a pinch, and then he Rebirth was pumped into her system. The sounds of the bells disappeared. Euphoria splashed all over her brain mixed with Serotonin. She smiled. Chill bumps appeared all over her body. Her heart began to pound like a bass drum. She bit into her bottom lip until she could taste blood. She wanted to die.

Stevo stroked her cheek. He leaned his head sideways, and kissed her lips. He stepped back, and fixed the covers on her. His eyes lowered. Cassidy's face came into his mind. To him, she was a threat. Cassidy *wanted* to take Jada away from him. *Selfish bitch*, he thought. *Always thinking of herself. What about what I want? Nobody gives a fuck about Stevo.* He became irate. He grabbed a syringe out of the top drawer. He slammed his arm on to the of the dresser, and injected himself. The powder form of the Rebirth had been failing to give him the kick that he'd been looking for. He wanted to become one with Jada. As soon as the drug coursed through his system, it turned him into a lunatic. His eyes were red. The beats of his heart sped up. He grew even more angry.

Cassidy came to the doorway. "Where is my daughter, Stevo? I need to get her to a hospital." She used the wall to keep her upright. She was bleeding profusely.

Stevo eyed her sinisterly. "So, you saying you wanna take my sister away from me? Is that it?"

Cassidy groaned as she made her way across the room. "Boy, ain't nobody trying to take this girl away from you. She needs help. You done fucked her up." She hurried to Jada's side.

Jada felt her heart stop. She opened her eyes wide. She sat up and took a deep breath. Her heart beat three hard times. Then it stopped again. She fell back, holding her chest. Her heart beat seven quick times. Then stopped for a second. It beat three more times, and stopped for three seconds. Her brain shut down. She pissed on herself. Everything went black. Then her heart began to beat over and over, rapidly. She rolled out of the bed and began to convulse on the carpet.

"You see." Cassidy knelt beside her. She turned Jada over. Foam began to come out of her mouth like soap suds. "What did you give her?" She screamed. Cassidy began to panic.

Stevo stood there in shock. "Save my sister! Please save her. Jada! I need you!" He knelt beside Cassidy.

Cassidy ripped Jada's shirt down the middle. "Sasha, bring me my purse off of that couch. Hurry up!"

Sasha had been watching at the door. She watched Jada shaking, and foaming at the mouth. She smiled. She hoped that Jada was on her way out of the Game. "Okay, Cassidy." She gingerly walked to the front room to grab the purse. She picked it up, and walked in the kitchen to pour herself a glass of water. She put her finger under the stream and waited until it was cold. Then she filled her cup with it. She took a sip, and laughed. "I hope that bitch die." She whispered.

"Did you find it?" Cassidy yelled.

"No, I'm still looking!" She lied. She poured on the glass of water, and filled her cup up again.

Stevo appeared in the doorway fuming. He watched Sasha dancing around, and laughing with her back to him. She played with the faucet as if she were a little kid. He closed the distance been them. Grabbed a handful of her hair and slammed her face into the refrigerator, knocking her out. He kicked her twice in the ribs, and picked the purse up from the kitchen floor. He hurried back into the bedroom.

Stevo handed Cassidy the purse. "Here, mama. Please, save my sister."

Cassidy paused for second. She was lost by the fact that he had called her mama. She melted. Then she was back focused on the task at hand. She took the Narcan out of her purse, and squirted the mist under Jada's nose. She squirt it twice. The drug worked immediately to reverse the effects of the overdose. Jada felt like her body was being turned inside out. She screamed, and began to shake harder. Slowly but surely the Narcan began to overpower the overdose until she was back to a normal state.

Cassidy jumped up and ran her a bathtub full of freezing cold water. "Stevo, bring her in here. Hurry up, baby."

Stevo carried her inside of the room, and lowered her into the tub. Jada' woke up as if she were being drowned.

She began to panic. She looked for an escape route out of the tub. Stevo held her down. "Be cool, sis. Please. This shit gotta come out of your system."

Jada continued to struggle until she became too weak. She laid back crying. Snot ran out of her nose. She released her bowels. She couldn't help it.

Cassidy shook her head. "I don't know what you did to this girl, but we have to get her to a hospital, Stevo. She is sick. If we don't, she could potentially die." Cassidy warned him. She didn't want Jada to die. She wanted to get the chance to get to know her daughter. She wanted to explain to her why she had given her up for adoption. She wanted them to build a relationship. She had always wondered what kind of a woman she had turned into, and where she was. Now that she had found her, she never wanted to lose her baby again.

"Cassidy, I'm telling you for the last time. We don't need you here. You can go on about yo business. Matter fact, get yo ass up." He stood and grabbed her by the arm.

Cassidy stood and jerked away from him. "Get off of me."

Stevo pushed her into the hallway. He stepped into it with her and closed the door. "What happened to Seth?"

"Boy, what?" Cassidy was taken off guard by his questioning.

"You heard me. What happened to him?"

Cassidy backed up. "He tried to kill me and Maisey, and I had to do what I had to do."

"So, what did you do?" Stevo bumped his chest into hers. He kept pushing her toward the front of the house. He wanted her out of Jada's house. He no longer wanted to be in her presence. The more he looked at her face the angrier he got.

"I stabbed his ass. I stabbed him before he could kill me. There. That's what happened." She admitted.

Stevo grabbed her by the throat and slung her into the living room. "Get yo shit and get the fuck out of here, bitch. Go find Makaroni. Go suck that nigga dick or something!" He spat.

Cassidy grabbed her purse and coat. She took one look to her right and saw Sasha laid out face-first on the kitchen floor. She shook her head and felt her stomach drop. Stevo was out of his mind. She was convinced. "Okay, Stevo, I'll go. But I'm telling you, son, if you don't get that girl to a hospital she is going to die. It'll be all your fault if that happens."

Stevo opened the front door and threw her onto the porch. "Bitch, you just worry about yourself. You ain't got no room to be giving me no orders or advice. Fuck off." He slammed the door in her face.

Cassidy stood in front of the closed door for a short while. She didn't know what her next move was going to be. Stevo was impossible to reason with. She exhaled in defeat. "All I can do is pray for him. Lord knows that's all I can do."

Stevo watched her get into her car. She sat in it for a moment staring at the house. Then she started her ignition and pulled away. He stepped away from the curtains. He walked over to a snoring Sasha and knelt beside her. He smacked her face hard. "Bitch, get up."

Sasha opened her eyes. Her jaw felt like it was broken. "Daddy, I'm sorry. I didn't mean to be hardheaded. I promise I'll do better."

Stevo frowned. "I'ma let Jada sleep for a few hours. While she sleep, you clean up this house, and run her some hot bath water. You hear me?"

Sasha lowered her head. She felt like scum. "Yes, Daddy. I got you."

Stevo yanked her up by her collar. He placed his face against hers. "If you ever pull a stunt like that again, I will take the breath out of your lungs for good. You understand me, Sasha?"

"Yes." She whimpered.

He pushed her away from him. "Good. Get this house in order. You're skating on thin ice."

Chapter 19

Two days later, on a stormy Friday night, rain fell hard from the sky like hail. It pelted against the roof top of Makaroni's Bentley truck. Lightning lit up the sky, followed by a boisterous rumbling of thunder. Makaroni checked the time on his cellphone. It read 8:09pm. He sat impatiently waiting for Stevo. The man had promised him that he would have met him a half hour ago. He closed his eyes and tried to calm himself.

Rubio Flores had been in contact with him twice since their last meeting. He wanted to light a fire under Makaroni's ass. Neither Phoenix nor JaMichael had come to an understanding. The war for supremacy in Memphis had gotten worst. It was so bad that the Mayor issued a seven o'clock curfew to all of its citizens within the Orange Mound and White Haven areas of the city. Shootings were up by fifty percent. The murder rate had skyrocketed. The Governor had been petitioned to bring in the national guard, and he was seriously considering it.

Makaroni knew that he had to go down and get a handle on things. Rubio had reminded him that if things weren't figured out by Sunday he would personally see to it that all Stevens' were crushed, and vanquished. Makaroni couldn't allow for that to happen. He needed for himself and Stevo to bind together to solve the problem. As much as he disliked some of the decisions that Stevo made, there was still nobody on earth that he felt he could solve the problem with other than Stevo. All it would take was for them to come to a solid understanding.

Makaroni squinted as Stevo pulled into the lot of the old railway station. His headlights beamed into Makaroni's eyes, dilating his pupils. "Damn, 'bout time his ass got here." He popped the lock on his passenger's door.

Stevo jogged through the rain. He pulled open the passenger's doors and slid into the seat. "What it do, fool?"

"Nigga, yo ass hella late. What the fuck took you so long?"

Stevo didn't like being questioned by nobody. He was a boss. To question a boss was unacceptable behavior. "Nigga, shit happens, but I'm here now. So, how we finna work this thang? Rubio hollered at me earlier today and said that he's over them two niggas. He said that if we crush them then he'll put us in their slots. We'll be the ones rolling Jags, and living in mansions and shit. I think that's long overdue, too."

"That's all you care about ain't it?" Makaroni asked him. Stevo looked skinnier to him. There were bags under his eyes. He could smell his cologne but he could tell that it was sprayed on an unwashed body. He felt bad for him.

"You damn right that's all I care about. Money make the mafuckin' world go 'round. You should know that. You remember how stuck our world was when we ain't have a pot to piss in. Remember how everybody used to shit on us? Damn, nigga. We were all that we had."

"Yeah, I remember all of that. And on some real shit, I'd rather go back to that life than to continue to live this one the way we are. Man, we done hurt so many people that it ain't even funny."

Stevo laughed. "Shit happens, nigga. You know how that goes. But anyway, we ain't here for all of that. What do you propose we do about them Jokers down south?" He looked out of his passenger's window. A big lightning bolt shot across the sky, illuminating the darkness for a split second. Thunder growled loudly as if the heavens were angry.

"I say we go down there and try to squash that shit. If we can get them on the same page then we can all eat comfortably."

"That's yo solution? A peace talk? Really?" He snickered. The Rebirth had him floating on Cloud 9.

"Yeah. We can't go down there just killing up mafuckas again. Them are my people. Especially Phoenix."

"Especially Phoenix? What you mean by that?"

Makaroni sighed. "I found out that Phoenix is my father; both mine and Montana's."

Stevo was cracking up. "So, the shysty ass leader of the Duffel Bag Cartel is your father? Really? Now, that's interesting." He slapped his lap laughing like an idiot.

Makaroni mugged him. "Anyway, that's why we can't kill him. And when it comes to JaMichael, that's my cousin. So we gotta come up with a better way to do things. We have to think outside of the box for once."

Stevo shook his head. "You got me fucked up. Them yo peoples. Not mine. You and that bitch Cassidy killed my old man, so why should I give a fuck about killing yours, or yo' punk ass cousin? Why, nigga?"

Makaroni held this silence for a few moments. "Look, I didn't kill Seth. I would have though had I gotten a hold of his punk ass. But I didn't get that chance. I don't feel sorry about his death though."

"Nigga, you said all of that to say what?" Stevo was getting more and more heated.

"I'm saying I think we should go down there and squash shit between them. Now that I know Phoenix is my pops, I'ma set up a meeting with him. My mother flew down there yesterday night. He already knows. He been blowing me up like crazy. It ain't gon' be nothin' to squash that shit now. My mother said that once she done hollering at Phoenix,

JaMichael is next. All we gotta do is go down there with a game plan to help her out. Pick up from where she left off."

Stevo nodded. "Yeah, all of that shit would sound fine if Rubio hadn't told me that if we crush them we can be the bosses. You already know how I get down. I don't like running under no nigga. Right now there are four niggas and their crews eating off of the Rebirth. That's way too many."

"So, what are you saying, Stevo? Fuck all of that beating around the bush. We either gon' figure this shit out as brothers, or it's gone all fall apart. We need to come back together. You are my nigga. I love you, dawg. Ever since this money came into play, shit ain't been right. What's it gon' be, bruh?"

Stevo shook his head. "There can only be one, Makaroni. I'm that nigga." He came from under his jacket with a Mach .90. He aimed at Makaroni and pulled the trigger. *Boom! Boom! Boom!*

The insides of the truck lit up as if fireworks were going off. Blood splattered all over the windshield. After emptying half of the clip, Stevo slammed the passenger's door. He jumped back into his whip and smashed away from the scene with a sadistic smile on his face.

***

Bomp! Bomp! Bomp!

Early the next morning, Montana was at Jada's house beating on the door with her closed fist. It was still raining outside. Mascara ran down her cheeks. She beat on the door again. "Stevo! Stevo, open the fuckin' door. I know you're in there." Montana turned around and eyed his Bentley truck that was parked in front of the house. It hadn't taken much for Montana to get the address out of Cassidy. She said that she was done with Stevo. That he was a lunatic and she wanted to stay as far away from him as she could. Montana beat some more.

Stevo rubbed the cold out of his eyes. He grabbed one of the two guns off of the dresser, and came down the hallway in just his boxers. Sasha opened her guestroom door, and stuck her head out of it. He walked right past her without saying a word. He looked out of the front window and saw Montana with mascara running down her face. He frowned and pulled the door open. "Bitch, who told you that I was here?"

Montana bumped her way into the house. "Who shot up my brother, Stevo? I know you know who did because you're always apart of everything evil!" She snapped.

Stevo turned his back on her. "Why the fuck y'all always blaming everything on me? I don't know shit about it." He laughed.

Montana felt her heart sink. She searched his face. Her eyes got bigger. "*You.* You did it. You did that to Makaroni? Why, Stevo? Why would you do that? He loved you like a brother." She dropped to her knees, crying at the revelation.

Stevo was disgusted. "Fuck Makaroni. That nigga was too soft for me. Ain't nobody gon' stand in the way of me becoming a true Drug Lord. Nobody. Money makes the muthafuckin' world go 'round, bitch. It's common fuckin' sense." He stared down at her. He put the gun to her head. "Get yo punk ass up and strip."

"Fuck you. You killed my brother and think I'ma strip for you? You got me twisted." She wiped away her tears.

"N'all, bitch, *you* got me twisted if you think you ain't." He grabbed her up by her hair and threw her to the couch. She fought him. He overpowered her easily. He yanked her skirt up and got between her thighs. He ripped her panties from her in one tug. He took his piece out of his boxer hole. "You gon' gimme this pussy, bitch. Makaroni ain't here to save you now." He searched her opening with his dick head.

It slipped between her lips, and then he was in. He humped fast and hard.

Montana screamed. She beat at his face. He lowered into her chest and kept going. She was hot and wet. He growled, still pumping.

"Get off of me."

Stevo sat up and pressed the gun to her forehead. "Bitch, shut up! Don't say shit else! I mean it." He roared. He waited for a moment, and then continued pumping hard with his eyes closed.

Sasha crept out of the hallway with a butcher's knife in her hand. She stood there for a moment. She looked back down hallway and saw Kandace appear out of the guestroom.

She'd called her and told her where Jada lived, and that Stevo would be there. She was tired of him. Tired of being treated like trash. Tired of giving her all, and getting nothing but abuse in return. She needed to find another way. Kandace promised her greener pastures if she agreed to set Stevo up, and work under her inside of her female Cartel that she was assembling. Kandace told her about her connection to the Rebirth. She told her about her plug into Makaroni and Montana. Kandace made it all sound so appealing to a broken Sasha. It didn't take long before she was convinced.

Sasha waited until Kandace was beside her. Kandace nodded at her. Sasha took a deep breath and scurried across the carpet. She raised the knife over her head, and plunged it into Stevo's spine as hard as she could. He froze, and dropped the gun. He fell off of Montana onto his side. Montana hurried away from him. She pulled her skirt down and hugged herself in the corner of the room.

Kandace ran over and aimed her Glock at him. "Yeah, nigga. Karma's a bitch ain't it?"

Stevo was shocked. He couldn't move his limbs. The knife had pierced a few of his nerves, paralyzing him. "Bitches! I'ma kill all of you bitches."

"Arrgh!" Sasha ran and jumped on him. She straddled him and began to stab him over and over again. All of the heartaches. All of the pain, it was all released through her arm, and the knife. She plunged it over and over. Hitting his face. His neck. His chest. Everywhere that she could think of to hurt him. When she stood up, Stevo laid shaking on the floor as if he was about to explode.

Jada staggered into the living room with Stevo's gun in her hand. She limped over, holding her stomach. When she got to him, she aimed the gun down at him. Blood spilled out of his face. "I wish I never met you!" She screamed. She aimed and pulled the trigger twice, killing Stevo. She dropped the gun, and fell to her knees.

Kandace stood over him. She remembered the last time she shot him up and minutes later he'd disappeared. She wasn't taking a chance this time. She placed her barrel to his forehead and pulled the trigger. His head exploded like a pumpkin. Only then was she satisfied.

***

Six months later...

Kandace stepped on the gas of her pink and black Tesla. It shot forward, and she smiled hard. "This what I'm talking about, Montana. Now we getting money. I always wanted one of these. I finally got it." She changed gears, and switched lanes on the highway. The Tesla hummed and shot forward like a rocket. The jolt sent a thrill through Kandace. She gripped the steering wheel harder. "Hell yeah!"

Montana allowed for her hair to blow in the wind. The drop top allowed for the sun to heat her skin just right. "Girl,

I told you that all it would take was for us to plug in with Jahliya and her people down south. My mama got them fools to squash that bullshit. The family is back on track. Now our Cartel is stronger than ever. The Stevens' own all the rights to the Rebirth, and Jada is still plugging us with those black-market body parts. It's about to be a cold summer." Montana laughed, drinking from her gold bottle of Moët. "You aiight back there, Sasha?"

Sasha adjusted the Draco on her lap. She was alert, and focused. Her long curly hair blew in the wind. "I'm good, and y'all better know that I'll follow my sisters wherever this road takes us." She meant that. "I can't wait to see Makaroni, though. I'm glad he pulled through. One day we gon' need his backing. I'm sure of that."

"Yeah, but now we're getting so much money that when he finally is up to it, we'll be able to put him on. Us girls, we got this. The game is ours." Montana held up her gold bottle.

"Who run the world?" Kandace hollered.

"Girls!" Both Montana and Sasha shouted in unison.

"You damn right!" Kandace laughed, stepping on the gas.

The End.

Submission Guideline

Submit the first three chapters of your completed manuscript to ldpsubmissions@gmail.com, subject line: Your book's title. The manuscript must be in a .doc file and sent as an attachment. Document should be in Times New Roman, double spaced and in size 12 font. Also, provide your synopsis and full contact information. If sending multiple submissions, they must each be in a separate email.

Have a story but no way to send it electronically? You can still submit to LDP/Ca$h Presents. Send in the first three chapters, written or typed, of your completed manuscript to:

LDP: Submissions Dept
Po Box 870494
Mesquite, Tx 75187

DO NOT send original manuscript. Must be a duplicate.

Provide your synopsis and a cover letter containing your full contact information.

Thanks for considering LDP and Ca$h Presents.

Coming Soon from Lock Down Publications/Ca$h Presents

BOW DOWN TO MY GANGSTA

By **Ca$h**

TORN BETWEEN TWO

By **Coffee**

THE STREETS STAINED MY SOUL **II**

By **Marcellus Allen**

BLOOD OF A BOSS **VI**

SHADOWS OF THE GAME II

By **Askari**

LOYAL TO THE GAME **IV**

By **T.J. & Jelissa**

A DOPEBOY'S PRAYER **II**

By **Eddie "Wolf" Lee**

IF LOVING YOU IS WRONG… **III**

By **Jelissa**

TRUE SAVAGE **VII**

MIDNIGHT CARTEL II

DOPE BOY MAGIC III

By **Chris Green**

BLAST FOR ME **III**

DUFFLE BAG CARTEL **IV**

HEARTLESS GOON **IV**

A SAVAGE DOPEBOY II

By **Ghost**

A HUSTLER'S DECEIT III

KILL ZONE **II**

BAE BELONGS TO ME III

SOUL OF A MONSTER III

By **Aryanna**

THE COST OF LOYALTY **III**

By **Kweli**

THE SAVAGE LIFE III

CHAINED TO THE STREETS II

By **J-Blunt**

KING OF NEW YORK V

COKE KINGS IV

BORN HEARTLESS IV

By **T.J. Edwards**

GORILLAZ IN THE BAY V

De'Kari

THE STREETS ARE CALLING II

Duquie Wilson

KINGPIN KILLAZ IV

STREET KINGS III

PAID IN BLOOD III

CARTEL KILLAZ IV

Hood Rich

SINS OF A HUSTLA II

ASAD

TRIGGADALE III

Elijah R. Freeman

KINGZ OF THE GAME V

Playa Ray
SLAUGHTER GANG IV
RUTHLESS HEART II
By Willie Slaughter
THE HEART OF A SAVAGE II
By Jibril Williams
FUK SHYT II
By Blakk Diamond
THE DOPEMAN'S BODYGAURD II
By Tranay Adams
TRAP GOD II
By Troublesome
YAYO III
A SHOOTER'S AMBITION II
By S. Allen
GHOST MOB
Stilloan Robinson
KINGPIN DREAMS II
By Paper Boi Rari
CREAM
By Yolanda Moore
SON OF A DOPE FIEND II
By Renta
FOREVER GANGSTA II
By Adrian Dulan
LOYALTY AIN'T PROMISED
By Keith Williams

THE PRICE YOU PAY FOR LOVE II

By Destiny Skai

THE LIFE OF A HOOD STAR

By Rashia Wilson

TOE TAGZ II

By Ah'Million

CONFESSIONS OF A GANGSTA II

By Nicholas Lock

PAID IN KARMA II

By **Meesha**

Available Now

RESTRAINING ORDER **I & II**

By **CA$H & Coffee**

LOVE KNOWS NO BOUNDARIES **I II & III**

By **Coffee**

RAISED AS A GOON I, II, III & IV

BRED BY THE SLUMS I, II, III

BLAST FOR ME I & II

ROTTEN TO THE CORE I II III

A BRONX TALE I, II, III

DUFFEL BAG CARTEL I II III

HEARTLESS GOON

A SAVAGE DOPEBOY

HEARTLESS GOON I II III

DRUG LORDS I II III

Ghost

By **Ghost**

LAY IT DOWN **I & II**

LAST OF A DYING BREED

BLOOD STAINS OF A SHOTTA I & II III

By **Jamaica**

LOYAL TO THE GAME

LOYAL TO THE GAME II

LOYAL TO THE GAME III

LIFE OF SIN I, II III

By **TJ & Jelissa**

BLOODY COMMAS I & II

SKI MASK CARTEL I II & III

KING OF NEW YORK I II,III IV

RISE TO POWER I II III

COKE KINGS I II III

BORN HEARTLESS I II III

By **T.J. Edwards**

IF LOVING HIM IS WRONG...I & II

LOVE ME EVEN WHEN IT HURTS I II III

By **Jelissa**

WHEN THE STREETS CLAP BACK I & II III

By **Jibril Williams**

A DISTINGUISHED THUG STOLE MY HEART I II & III

LOVE SHOULDN'T HURT I II III IV

RENEGADE BOYS I II III IV

PAID IN KARMA

By **Meesha**

A GANGSTER'S CODE I &, II III

A GANGSTER'S SYN I II III

THE SAVAGE LIFE I II

CHAINED TO THE STREETS

By J-Blunt

PUSH IT TO THE LIMIT

By **Bre' Hayes**

BLOOD OF A BOSS **I, II, III, IV, V**

SHADOWS OF THE GAME

By **Askari**

THE STREETS BLEED MURDER **I, II & III**

THE HEART OF A GANGSTA I II& III

By **Jerry Jackson**

CUM FOR ME

CUM FOR ME 2

CUM FOR ME 3

CUM FOR ME 4

CUM FOR ME 5

An **LDP Erotica Collaboration**

BRIDE OF A HUSTLA **I II & II**

THE FETTI GIRLS **I, II& III**

CORRUPTED BY A GANGSTA I, II III, IV

BLINDED BY HIS LOVE

THE PRICE YOU PAY FOR LOVE

By **Destiny Skai**

WHEN A GOOD GIRL GOES BAD

By **Adrienne**

Ghost

THE COST OF LOYALTY I II

By Kweli

A GANGSTER'S REVENGE **I II III & IV**

THE BOSS MAN'S DAUGHTERS

THE BOSS MAN'S DAUGHTERS II

THE BOSSMAN'S DAUGHTERS III

THE BOSSMAN'S DAUGHTERS IV

THE BOSS MAN'S DAUGHTERS **V**

A SAVAGE LOVE **I & II**

BAE BELONGS TO ME I II

A HUSTLER'S DECEIT I, II, III

WHAT BAD BITCHES DO I, II, III

SOUL OF A MONSTER I II

KILL ZONE

By **Aryanna**

A KINGPIN'S AMBITON

A KINGPIN'S AMBITION **II**

I MURDER FOR THE DOUGH

By **Ambitious**

TRUE SAVAGE

TRUE SAVAGE II

TRUE SAVAGE **III**

TRUE SAVAGE **IV**

TRUE SAVAGE **V**

TRUE SAVAGE **VI**

DOPE BOY MAGIC I, II

MIDNIGHT CARTEL

By **Chris Green**

A DOPEBOY'S PRAYER

By **Eddie "Wolf" Lee**

THE KING CARTEL **I, II & III**

By **Frank Gresham**

THESE NIGGAS AIN'T LOYAL **I, II & III**

By **Nikki Tee**

GANGSTA SHYT **I II &III**

By **CATO**

THE ULTIMATE BETRAYAL

By **Phoenix**

BOSS'N UP **I , II & III**

By **Royal Nicole**

I LOVE YOU TO DEATH

By Destiny J

I RIDE FOR MY HITTA

I STILL RIDE FOR MY HITTA

By **Misty Holt**

LOVE & CHASIN' PAPER

By **Qay Crockett**

TO DIE IN VAIN

SINS OF A HUSTLA

By **ASAD**

BROOKLYN HUSTLAZ

By **Boogsy Morina**

BROOKLYN ON LOCK I & II

By **Sonovia**

GANGSTA CITY

By **Teddy Duke**

A DRUG KING AND HIS DIAMOND I & II III

A DOPEMAN'S RICHES

HER MAN, MINE'S TOO I, II

CASH MONEY HO'S

By Nicole Goosby

TRAPHOUSE KING **I II & III**

KINGPIN KILLAZ I II III

STREET KINGS I II

PAID IN BLOOD **I II**

CARTEL KILLAZ I II III

By **Hood Rich**

LIPSTICK KILLAH **I, II, III**

CRIME OF PASSION I II & III

By **Mimi**

STEADY MOBBN' **I, II, III**

THE STREETS STAINED MY SOUL

By **Marcellus Allen**

WHO SHOT YA **I, II, III**

SON OF A DOPE FIEND

Renta

GORILLAZ IN THE BAY **I II III IV**

DE'KARI

TRIGGADALE I II

Elijah R. Freeman

GOD BLESS THE TRAPPERS I, II, III

THESE SCANDALOUS STREETS I, II, III

FEAR MY GANGSTA I, II, III

THESE STREETS DON'T LOVE NOBODY I, II

BURY ME A G I, II, III, IV, V

A GANGSTA'S EMPIRE I, II, III, IV

THE DOPEMAN'S BODYGAURD

Tranay Adams

THE STREETS ARE CALLING

Duquie Wilson

MARRIED TO A BOSS... I II III

By Destiny Skai & Chris Green

KINGZ OF THE GAME I II III IV

Playa Ray

SLAUGHTER GANG I II III

RUTHLESS HEART

By Willie Slaughter

THE HEART OF A SAVAGE

By Jibril Williams

FUK SHYT

By Blakk Diamond

DON'T F#CK WITH MY HEART I II

By Linnea

ADDICTED TO THE DRAMA I II III

By Jamila

YAYO I II

A SHOOTER'S AMBITION

By S. Allen

TRAP GOD

By Troublesome

FOREVER GANGSTA

By Adrian Dulan

TOE TAGZ

By Ah'Million

KINGPIN DREAMS

By Paper Boi Rari

CONFESSIONS OF A GANGSTA

By Nicholas Lock

BOOKS BY LDP'S CEO, CA$H

TRUST IN NO MAN

TRUST IN NO MAN 2

TRUST IN NO MAN 3

BONDED BY BLOOD

SHORTY GOT A THUG

THUGS CRY

THUGS CRY 2

THUGS CRY 3

TRUST NO BITCH

TRUST NO BITCH 2

TRUST NO BITCH 3

TIL MY CASKET DROPS

RESTRAINING ORDER

RESTRAINING ORDER 2

IN LOVE WITH A CONVICT

Coming Soon

BONDED BY BLOOD 2

BOW DOWN TO MY GANGSTA

Ghost